# TOUCHES THE SKY

≈ *A Novel* ≈

# JAMES CALVIN SCHAAP

D0103711

Fleming H. Revell
A Division of Baker Book House Co
Grand Rapids, Michigan 49516

© 2003 by James Calvin Schaap

Published by Fleming H. Revell
a division of Baker Book House Company
P.O. Box 6287, Grand Rapids, MI 49516-6287
www.bakerbooks.com

Second printing, November 2003

Printed in the United States of America

Library of Congress Cataloging-in-Publication Data
Schaap, James C., 1948–
    Touches the sky : a novel / James Calvin Schaap.
        p.    cm.
    ISBN 0-8007-5892-7
    1. Immigrants—Fiction. 2. Dutch Americans—Fiction. 3. Dakota Ter-
ritory—Fiction. I. Title.
PS3569.C33T68  2003
813′.54—dc21                                                    2003007262

For the many thousands of descendants of nineteenth-century settlers, who, like my own immigrant Dutch great-grandparents, found homes and raised families on the Great Plains, on land that once belonged to the buffalo and a free and noble people.

May all of us come to understand more of their story.

## ❦ One ❧

I have decided to tell you the story, every part that remains in my memory. It does not haunt me, but to say I have not thought about it would be a lie, because it returns, every December, in the touch of winter's first wind. My memory retells it each time I see a leaden sky over a gray and parched land. A certain frightened pitch in the song of the meadowlark brings back whole chapters, and in the driving snow, images still appear in my memory like rigid, frozen ghosts.

To me, the story you want to hear is in the wind that blows unceasingly on this land where I have chosen to live. But I will tell you, because in part it is surely my own story too. And it begins with a funeral, and a trip across the Missouri.

She was right, of course—my wife was. Going all the way to the church at Friesland for a funeral—for this funeral—seemed somehow too generous, given the circumstances of this young man's death and the fact that he was not someone I knew. But I hadn't been east across the river for a long while, and I could afford to take the time. I had my reasons too, even if not all of them were particularly understandable to Dalitha—and not to me either, if I thought about it much.

There was this matter of the truth, after all. What exactly had happened to the young man who had died, Dries Balkema? It was November, 1890, and for months there'd been no hostile activity in the settlements east of the reservation. And while I knew many of the settlers spent their lives paralyzed by fear of what might be happening among the Sioux—most everyone had heard reports of this latest madness—most of those who knew Arie Boon doubted his story of the death of his hired man because they doubted Arie Boon. Even Boon's neighbors, even those with whom he went to church, were far less sure of him than they were of the bands of Sioux who wandered east from the reservation to trade for food or provisions.

Dries Balkema had come to Dakota Territory by himself—no family. At first, he and Boon seemed something of a good match, Dries being strong-willed and built for the hard work Boon would demand. It didn't take long, however, before most people knew of a growing rift between them. But then Boon was a man as harsh as the land he farmed.

The Sioux had come for horses, he'd said. They'd come when he wasn't around, and they killed Balkema while trying to get livestock. That was the story: Dries Balkema felled by what seemed a single bullet, no sign of a struggle.

8

Once east of the hills along the Missouri River, the land flattens like a long flag unfurled, brown as buckskin beneath the unending blue of heaven. So often back then, I couldn't help but think how remarkable it was that this vast sea of grass was being drawn and quartered. Everywhere buildings were rising in the area around the Friesland settlement.

When I'd first come to Dakota territory, some settlers had warned me about losing my way on the prairie. In a world so fully shorn of any distraction—no trees, no frame structures—a half-hour's walk could leave a man or a woman or even a horse disoriented. It could nearly hypnotize you, this endless ocean of grass and sky.

But settlements had arisen from the waves of grassland—here and there some squared humps of furry sod, now and then a frame house, a barn, a pencil line of trees promising, someday, a windbreak. Settlers were burrowing in, so many that it would be hard to get lost anymore in Charles Mix County.

Many were Hollanders, just come to this country and determined to do what no one, not even the Sioux, had ever done: put down roots on the wide open plains. But houses and barns, coops and sheds notwithstanding, a man or a woman could still become disoriented on the prairie, and that's what people feared about Balkema.

Arie Boon claimed he'd found him beside the fence south of the barn, a single bullet in his otherwise untouched body. Two horses were gone—but the animals were invalids, people said. Not even the Sioux would have taken them.

"Did you know the man?" Dalitha said as I'd pulled on my jacket earlier that morning. When I shook my head, she did as well. "Just exactly what good does it do, your going to that funeral? He has no family here, this man. Who needs your sympathy? Certainly not him, and certainly not this Boon—not by the way you describe him."

Dalitha always had an opinion, and usually she was right.

"You'll make Boon seem a martyr, that's what." She took my lapels in her hands. "Just your presence there, it will somehow strengthen his alibi, and you know it. Your very presence, from all the way across the river, will make the whole story seem somehow more credible." She shook her head. "What's strange about you, Jan, is that for a man of so little faith, you have so much commitment." She reached up and kissed me. "Promise me this: You won't say a word of comfort to this man Arie Boon."

For a woman with so much commitment, Dalitha Ward, my wife, found it uncommonly easy to dislike people. Boon blamed Balkema's death on the Indians Dalitha loved; if she were district judge, she wouldn't believe Arie Boon's story if he swore on a stack of Bibles and had a dozen blameless witnesses who'd seen him singing psalms in Sunday worship. That's where we differed, my wife and I. For all I knew, Arie Boon could have been right—it could have been the Sioux.

Amazing, isn't it, that with so much open sky, secrets could exist. But I'd lived on the grasslands long enough to hold on to at least this much of what I considered my father's faith—there was sufficient darkness in humankind to stretch all the way around the belly of the earth.

It was a radiant morning, but I remember what I felt was fear. Not, like the Sioux, simply from the unending march of white settlers west; many of the newcomers were my own people, after all. But something in my heart tore to pieces when I saw the land broken and harnessed. What I shared with the Sioux was the fear of a future that could not be imagined. No one knew what was going to happen here—not the Sioux, not the settlers, not even the deeply committed, like Dalitha, the ones who thought they knew the will of God. And there were many of those. But truthfully, no one knew what this land would become, and the not knowing, that's what I believed was most fearful.

Maybe that's why I felt I had to go to the funeral. I wasn't one of the Hollanders anymore, but they were still my people, even though I'd married an American of a wholly different faith. Part of me was still there in the open land around the Friesland church. Maybe I feared being lost—not eternally, but lost here, in a place some still called the "frontier."

Men like Arie Boon felt nothing of that. Boon would make it in Dakota or die trying, and he had sons born of the same mettle; they wouldn't disappear, miragelike, as some had who'd come and already left. Sometimes back then, when I'd be with Broken Antler or Sam Spotted

Horse in Old Platte, we would watch a man like Arie Boon beat up his kid for running off when he should've been loading the wagon. At moments like that I knew the Sioux understood that white settlers would change life forever out here, because the Arie Boons—be they Dutch or Norwegian or American—would hang on to this land until their fingers bled; they'd cut the earth's flesh into bits and pieces to reign like despots over a thousand square-cut grassland fiefdoms.

Most people in the Dutch settlements east of the river didn't doubt for a moment that Arie Boon had killed Dries Balkema, if not in actuality then by working him to death. After all, if there were hostiles about, how was it no one else had seen them? The land held few hiding places. Besides, the Sioux made convenient scapegoats.

Maybe they were alike, Boon and the hostiles he blamed, both commandeered by the firm conviction that nothing mattered but their own worlds, both driven by the jagged will to survive.

But Boon's visions didn't arise from his faith, as did the Indians'. Arie Boon had to break his faith—his Christian faith—to hold on; and he would, just as he would break anything and anyone else that stood in the path toward attaining a kingdom. That's what people knew—both settlers and Sioux.

It may well not have been hostiles from the Rosebud reservation who'd killed Dries Balkema; far more likely, people thought, it was the hostile in Arie Boon.

12

I was working as a drayman back then, a freighter, a teamster, running goods and provisions and even people back and forth across the Missouri, back and forth, to and from the Rosebud agency from the east, the Dutch Reformed colonies where I'd lived, and from the south, Valentine, Nebraska.

I'd come to Dakota running, you might say, eager to get away from a life that ended with the death of just about everything I'd held dear. For two years I'd stayed in western Charles Mix County with a brand-new community of people like myself, Hollanders, although most of them were immigrants. Then, in part because I had nothing to keep me there and in part because the work west of the river was far more lucrative, I'd left Friesland and Nieveen, just as I'd left Michigan, just as I'd left Iowa, and just as I'd left the church.

On the Rosebud reservation I met Dalitha Ward, and we surprised each other and ourselves by falling in love while stranded alone for three days in a wretched and blessed Dakota blizzard, then getting married when both of us understood that we had not even the remotest desire not to. But that's another story.

That morning in mid-November, on my way to the church at Friesland for the funeral of Dries Balkema, I met a wagon full of people silhouetted against the bright eastern sky. A pair of healthy horses out front blocked the driver at first—his hat was pulled down low over his forehead. That the family was white went without saying—maybe it was the hats, the caps. Then again, maybe

13

it was the direction of the wagon—west. I put the reins against my horse's neck and led her off the road to let the wagon pass.

"Ellerbroek," the driver said, half standing in the wagon. *"Wo ist?"*

It was Evert Hammersma, an old friend for whom I'd worked. He looked to be trucking some immigrants out somewhere west. "Got Swedes here," he said in the Dutch language. "Dumb as a box of rocks. Don't know a word of English."

Even though the sun was at his back, I looked up at him with the kind of squint everyone out here has from trying to make a living where you need always to watch the sky.

Like so many, the people he was toting were completely unacquainted with the place, brand new to America and still clothed like Europeans—wool pants, caps, coats.

"They have relatives?" I asked.

Evert pointed north and west. "Should have put them on a train, but they got no money," he said. "Just call me an angel of mercy."

"Good Samaritan," I said.

"That too. Whatever will get me in the Good Book."

I told him that would take a lot more than one trip, and he laughed. The little girl's perfectly red cheeks already spoke of too much sun. I came up close on my horse and tugged the edge of her cap down slightly over her forehead, teasing. "She's beautiful," I told her mother.

14

"They don't understand a word," Evert said, but the woman smiled. "Got business in town?" he asked.

"Balkema," I said.

"May he rest in peace," Evert grumbled, pulling out a pipe. "That's more than he ever got from Arie." Then he laughed, giggled, like he sometimes did. "Some say he's better off, poor guy."

He jammed that pipe in his mouth and flicked a match against the side of the box. "You know, Jan, my mother, she prays every day even now for your spiritual health. I tell her he made his own bed when he married that American woman." He winked teasingly.

The father of the Swedish family barely looked at me, but the mother, her hair falling from her scarf in golden ringlets, had strong eyes. Maybe she could do it, I thought. I could picture her with a shotgun or a pitchfork.

"Early winter this year?" Evert said.

I told him every winter was early in Dakota, even though that one—1890—wouldn't be.

"You wonder sometime," he said, half turning. "You know, even I get a sour belly from this work." He thumbed at his human cargo. "What do they know about living out here? Look here," he said, swinging his arm back. "It's all they got—in those trunks there—two of them. Well, we all got to start somewhere, I guess, don't we? You and me, Jan, we did it too."

"They've got family?" I said again.

Evert nodded. "Who can tell for sure? It's what they claim." Then he stood to get out some kinks, but he really didn't want his cargo to hear. "You know, I don't like going this direction," he said, looking west toward the reservation. "Too many rumors maybe."

"They're the ones who scare me, Evert," I told him, nodding toward the family. "You and me, we'll make it. They're like lambs to the slaughter, eh?"

"Hostiles?" Evert asked.

I meant the difficulty of making a life out here, but Hammersma was talking about the Sioux. And the truth was that even though Little Big Horn, the Battle of Greasy Grass, was years ago already, there was always something to fear about the Sioux. Whether Dalitha liked it or not, white people kept coming every week back then; numbers was all it took to make something end, more people looking for something they couldn't have in the old country, something they would eventually take forever from the Sioux. We didn't think of what we were doing as taking anything that belonged to anyone—no white people thought of homesteading in that way, not that family in the wagon and not the Hollanders among whom I'd lived. No white folks understood that, except maybe Dalitha and a few others who lived long enough among the Sioux to have something of a Dacohtah heart beating in their own chests.

"Do we got to worry?" Evert asked me.

"How would you feel?" I said. "The buffalo are gone and so is their land." I tried to smile because it was an issue that could go up like a prairie fire.

16

Evert held out a hand as if he held a loaf of something still steaming. "I'm no farmer either. You know, in Holland my father was a baker, but he built a farm in Iowa." He took a deep breath, as if the aroma was still in the air. "You tell me, Jan, who of us hasn't had to change, and why should it be any different for them? Let 'em raise hogs like the rest of us—that's where the future is out here. Sooner or later we'll all be pig farmers, eh?" He snorted like a sow then turned to the wagon. "He just doesn't know it yet." He rubbed his hand over his face. "But tell me, Jan, what's the story with this new crazy dance? Is it true?"

"Depends on what you've heard."

"It makes them crazy, that's what's going around," Evert said, signaling with his hand as if to say the rumors were thick. "It's a kind of madness, and hate too—lots of hate." He pointed back down the road. "People are scared back there."

"Did you tell them?" I said, nodding toward the immigrant family.

"I'll let their own people do that," he said, shrugging his shoulders. He pulled himself up in the seat. "You'll be asked, you know. People will want to know what's happening across the river." Evert wasn't lying—fear was in his face. "You've seen it yourself maybe, this messiah madness?"

"It's like their church," I told him. "The Sioux don't come to your church, and we don't go to theirs."

"Then what do you hear?"

I looked at the people huddled in the wagon, naïve, blind to fierce Dakota life, yet optimistic. You could see it in the woman's eyes. We all had to have faith to live—settlers and Sioux, farmers and city dwellers. We all had to believe in something.

"There's little to worry about," I told Evert, but that was a half-truth, like his own. "It's just their faith, you know. It's the Sioux religion. It's only what they do when they dance."

Evert didn't understand.

"Just like Hollanders," I said. "It's just what they do when they go to church. Don't think they all believe it, eh?"

Evert looked at the horses as if offended. Maybe that was one step too far.

I turned to the woman in the wagon. "Home?" I said, smiling, pointing west.

"*Ja,*" the woman said, nodding.

"What does she know?" Evert said in Dutch.

But the woman had fierce eyes that I knew even the Sioux would fear.

18

# ≈ *Two* ≈

"I need to speak to you afterwards," Mrs. Boon told me as I came up to the church. Deliberately, it seemed, she'd left her family to seek me out. "Not now," she said, her hand on my arm. "Don't leave without stopping. Promise me."

"What is it?" I said.

She looked around as if there were far too many open ears, then stuttered as if she didn't know exactly how to start. "It's not the place or time right now," she said. "But there's things that got to be said, Jan. You can't leave without stopping."

And then she walked away, her family on the steps of the church, her husband, Arie, looking back at her—at the two of us—menacingly.

I had meant to talk to Arie Boon anyway, to try to get to the truth. It was part of the reason I'd come. It still seemed unlikely that the Sioux had killed Boon's hired man, but if so, someone on the reservation should know

19

about it. And something in the way Arie's wife had said what she did, the urgency, made me think there was more to the story. But then I knew that few of those who were gathering that morning for the funeral would have thought any less.

I don't know that you have any idea about the world I'm talking about right now—I mean where I was just then, and what I'd come from. Friesland, in the brand-new state of South Dakota, was no more of a village than any of a number of settlements back then, a few years after the first white settlers had moved to the wide open spaces just east of the Missouri River. Friesland was a church— that's all. But the church stood at the heart of the immigrant settlement of Dutch people—Frisians, actually— that was as close to the Missouri River as any of the communities Hollanders had created in the 1880s. For the most part, those who worshipped there were immigrants, although there were always others moving in and out, most of them, like myself, struck with something of the pioneer spirit, I guess. Many of those came from Iowa, where land was already at a premium; back then, Dakota land was either homesteaded or else sold so cheaply that a man could buy half a township for a good pair of horses. Some people, like Dries Balkema, came west from even farther away—Wisconsin or Michigan.

I wasn't there in 1882 when those Frieslanders got together and decided to worship for the first time, but they were always proud of the story, how they'd determined to hold worship at the only school in the area but

20

then arrived on Sunday morning and found the place occupied by Lutherans. It never occurred to them to worship together; of course, they wouldn't have understood a word of Norwegian. More important, probably, they were not Lutheran, they were True Dutch Reformed. So they simply stepped back up into their wagons and drove to an open meadow, circled up the rigs, and praised the Lord beneath the open sky. Of that story they were proud.

Friesland was a community of hardscrabble immigrant farmers trying to find a way to stay alive in that harsh country, and almost always calling on the help of the Lord. And you ought to know this too—sometimes they had absolutely nothing else. What I'm saying is, the hub, the heart of it all, was the church.

I can't guess how much you might know about the people Dries Balkema came from, but maybe I can't explain them better than I just did.

The church where I was bound that morning was just a year old, and it stood where its predecessor had since the first Friesland church had been built five years earlier in 1884, two years after those settlers worshipped for the first time on the prairie grass. But that church building had been destroyed by fire in 1889, two days before Christmas. This new one, people were proud to say, was financed in part by a check for $400 from the denomination, half a continent away in Michigan. People were proud of that too, maybe because it made them believe they weren't alone beneath a sky that sometimes seems so oversized there could be no one else there.

Only a modest bell tower distinguished the building as a house of worship; it was a frame church, almost square, very small, not at all unlike a country school. But it stood high on the land, and when that bell sounded on Sunday morning, its ring and the open land around it meant men and women and children miles away would hear it and begin to gather.

That morning, the morning of Dries Balkema's funeral, the new church was full. One of the Zylstra boys—I think it was Bert—looked up when I sat beside him, nodded politely, but didn't say a thing, respecting the silence. It was the passionate seriousness of the Hollanders that Dalitha couldn't take, especially in church. It was as if, she'd say, simply a word to a neighbor would get you blotted from the Book of Life. She'd joke about every last service being funeral-like; but what I attended that morning *was* a funeral, a funeral of a very special type.

Dries Balkema wasn't much more than a kid, really, and he had no family anywhere near. I didn't know him. I wish I had. His death seemed a double tragedy, I think, because loneliness was a persistent ailment most people suffered from, with the exception, of course, of those who, like Dries's boss, Arie Boon, rarely seemed to look up into the open sky. But I knew that very few of those who attended Balkema's funeral bought Boon's Indian story; most of them simply assumed Dries's death had occurred in the kind of heated confrontation Boon was known to create out of nothing at all.

That's why there was something dubious about Boon and his wife sitting up front that morning as if they were a loving family. Most assumed Arie Boon to be somehow the cause of Dries's death, the whole Indian story an alibi created to protect him from the accusation that it was his own sheer brutality that had taken the life of his hired man.

That Friesland church was almost brand new, like so much else in those early settlements, so for me at least there were no memories there, nothing inside the sanctuary to remind me of ever having been there before. Even the organ was new, bigger than the little one they'd used when I'd lived there, the one some family had brought along from Iowa. There was no particular pain for me in that building, even though I knew one of the reasons I'd come back had to do with a death I'd tried not to remember.

Less than ten years had passed since Mr. LeCocq, their leader, and a number of others had found open land in central Douglas County, a day's ride east—maybe less— from the Missouri River. Once they had agreed on where they wanted to settle, they hung an empty oyster can from a plaster lath stuck in the ground to distinguish their claim as a place for Hollanders to live. In just a few years, a whole series of communities had grown around that plaster lath, far more than a thousand people come to live in all that openness, to start new lives in their old wooden shoes. When that land filled up with newcomers, the only thing to do was to keep moving toward reservation land. Friesland, where I'd come to live, in Charles Mix County just a stone's throw from the Missouri, was one of the Dutch colonies farthest west.

Maybe I talk too much. Maybe you're saying right now that I talk way too much. But it's all part of the story you want to hear, and to say much less is not to tell it at all. It seems to me that I have lived long enough now not to have to lie anymore. So you're going to get everything I remember, as it stays with me and God gives me the patience to tell it.

I was surprised to see Abraham De Vries ascend the pulpit that morning, not a preacher. Rev. Bode was in Minnesota, working, I was told later. The harvest had been bad that summer. Bad? There'd been nothing, and the dominie was in Minnesota because without crops there was no money; without money, he had no salary. That too was something Dalitha didn't understand, that sometimes the settlers found life no less difficult for themselves than it was for the Sioux—maybe even more so, because for them there were no government provisions and annuities.

"Dearly beloved," De Vries said in the Frisian language, reading even the familiar words from a tablet held up close to his eyes. "We are gathered here . . ."

And then, even though the church was new, even though the Dakota landscape had no trees like the Michigan lakeshore, even though I was more than ten long years older now, and even though I was married once again, I felt myself lifted back to another frame church

24

where I'd stood alone, my first wife's body just outside in a funeral wagon. And my father—my own father—reading the words of Psalm 68 as a priceless treasure passionately kept, each word savored as if together the solemn phrases were some divine elixir.

I don't believe in ghosts, but after sixty-some years I believe that the spirits of difficult things are never really buried once and for all on this side of eternity. What I hadn't come home for was the memory that opened in me right there in the Friesland church, as unforeseen as a white buffalo, as oppressive as a moonless sky once it returned again.

When the funeral began, everyone stood. I had no Psalter, so Zylstra offered to share his. We sang Psalm 116, of course. I held the corner of Zylstra's book, but I didn't need to see the words because I must have sung Psalm 116 a thousand times, most often as a child not thinking of what he was singing.

But what came back to me then was the unforgettable moment when I stood alone in the front of a small church in Michigan, my wife and baby gone, like our precious daughter already laid into the earth. That memory came back with the force of a wind I couldn't withstand, and I couldn't sing the words of that old psalm, I couldn't. "He hears my voice, my cry and supplication; inclines His ear . . ."

I couldn't sing, because I remembered the moment when I'd felt something beneath me give way completely. I remembered my father up behind the pulpit—"No need

25

for a *voorsanger* with Dominie Ellerbroek," people used to say—my father standing up in front of everyone as if robed in the glories of Zion, not with a smile because a smile would've been unthinkable, but with his deep jaw squarely set with confidence, a confidence that I, his own son, couldn't hope for. "In life, in death my heart will seek His face," my father said, with not a taste of the doubt that drowned my soul.

There I stood in the new church in Friesland, remembering another funeral, because even though I'd married again, even though my life had found new meaning west of the Missouri River, even though I'd felt happiness again, I could not forget that part of my life when God's Word had burned my heart. As a young man, I could sing as lustily as Bert Zylstra did that day, with my first wife and daughter beside me, all of us Sabbath clean and standing in a church with the other saints. I had believed what the words said, or at least trusted that should something happen someday, they would be eternally true: "The Lord is just, His grace wide as the ocean; In boundless mercy He fulfills His word." In a life unbroken, belief is a sure thing.

And then Rinska died in childbirth—both of them died. And nothing about God and love and his rule in my life made any sense. There was nothing left for me in Michigan, so I went west, first to Iowa, where there were already too many holy and righteous people, and then to South Dakota, where the backbreaking work of making a life offered precious little time for pretension and self-righteousness.

26

It wasn't always true in my father's churches, but in Dakota Territory, for some reason—maybe it was the life all of them had lived in a soddie, a home like a badger's— the men and women sat together in worship, although not "together" as they would have in Dalitha's church. Together in the sense that they weren't on opposite sides, as they always were in Michigan and Iowa. That day in Friesland, the women sat in the middle—there were no children at the funeral—and the men sat around them, as if for protection, like a windbreak. I was happy to stand there on the outside, on the edge, on the very edge, so close to the outside that I could leave at any moment, just as I'd left Michigan after Rinska's death, just as I'd left the Friesland settlement, just as I'd left the circle of their steadfast faith.

> Thou, O Jehovah, in Thy sovereign grace
> Hath saved my soul from death and woe appalling.

That boy of Zylstra sang with sure knowledge and a firm confidence, the same certainty I'd seen in my father's eyes and set jaw at the funeral of my wife and child.

> Dried all my tears, secured my feet from falling;
> Lo, I shall live and walk before Thy face.

Zylstra's voice rose like a sandhill crane into a warm blue sky, and I remember it painfully because I could make no such music.

And then, suddenly, I heard my own voice in the psalm:

27

I have believed, and therefore did I speak
When I was made to suffer tribulation.
I said in haste and bitter desperation;
All men are false, 'tis nought but lies they speak.

Suddenly it seemed to me as if every mile I'd traveled between Friesland and the reservation was undertaken so that the God of Israel, the God of my father, the Lord God of hosts could let me hear the sound of my own voice coming from his Word. I couldn't help but believe that he was telling me that he knew the doubt in my mind.

There were times back then when the God of the universe struck me with fear, not so much because of his wrath, but because of what my father would call his omnipresence, his never, ever being gone, even if I wished him to be. I'd run from his face, but often I'd see him in sunsets, in steep winds whose feet ran in shifting currents across fields of prairie grass. That morning, at the funeral of a young man I barely knew, God Almighty spoke to me in my own rebellious voice: "I said in haste and bitter desperation; all men are false, 'tis nought but lies they speak."

I'd come to understand that nothing I would do or see or experience could ever be perceived without some reference to the sovereign God of my father and my own childhood. How did the catechism say it?—"neither life nor death shall separate me . . ." Faith was planted in the very hidden corners of my soul, whether or not I gave my consent. No matter how hard I argued, even here in the bare openness of a place that seemed to hold no shelter, with a sky as big as anything I'd ever seen, in moments of silence—and there were many—I knew I could never escape the presence of a God who was over me always. I didn't love him, but I knew he would never leave me alone.

"Jerusalem! Within thy courts I'll praise Jehovah's name," Zylstra sang, but all the way through that hymn, I didn't open my mouth, even though every phrase sang somehow in me.

After the funeral, I spoke to the man who'd led it— Abraham De Vries—and I said what everyone was saying, that Dries Balkema was too young to be put into the ground. De Vries, hat in his hand, asked me why I'd come.

"I came to tell you," I said, "this business of the hostiles—it's not something to fear. If it was some young buck, you shouldn't think it something widespread."

The two of us stood near our horses, just a stone's throw from the ground where Dries Balkema had been laid. The people who'd come to the gravesite were slowly dispersing in silence.

"You needn't worry," De Vries said. "There are more things to fear in all of this than Indians." With his hat, he tapped his own chest, his own heart, then put it back on his head, his Bible still under his arm. "Faithfulness," he said, "obedience—we need it more and more out here and see it less and less." Then he looked at me closely. "But Jan," he said, "tell me what is happening on the reservation."

"Takes a heart of steel not to feel some pity," I told him. "Hundreds more people out here every time I turn around. The whole place bustles like a city."

"And they have their place too, don't they, the Sioux? The government gives them their place."

"This is their place," I said. "All of this was their place."

He took the Bible from beneath his arm and held it out. "And it's our place to bring them this, Jan. You don't agree?"

"You're more sure than I am," I said.

He was shocked. "To bring the gospel to every land?" he said. "That's what our Lord commanded—his last words on this earth. Even your wife's people don't deny that."

I told him that taking away their land and giving them a book in its place seemed something less than a bargain to the Sioux. De Vries looked away into the horizon, angry at my unbelief.

It would be easy to say that the Sioux would have had less to fear if there were more Abraham De Vrieses than Arie Boons in Charles Mix County. That would be easy to say, but I'm not sure it would have been true. De Vries's faith, like Boon's industry, was made of toughest metal.

Dries Balkema was buried on Arie Boon's land, very much alone, beneath a stand of cottonwoods in a hilly cleft, where there would be no tombstone because there was no money and no immediate family. No one would remember him, I thought.

In those first years, when I regularly drove to the railroad, I'd often search for the grave of Opke Reinsma, an old man who'd come all the way from the old country with his children's families. Three days of rain forced them to sleep in the Plankington railroad station and wait for the mud roads to dry so they could finally get to their new home. Unexpectedly, death came to Opke, who, like Moses, people said, had breathed his last while close enough to see the Promised Land. He'd been buried in a box outside of a town that, like so many others, had sprung up overnight, and the location of the site was soon lost. The Reinsmas begged me to look for it on my trips, and I had, but I never found the spot, and it's likely no one ever will. Opke's family saw him singing with the angels, I'm sure, but that assurance didn't comfort the hurt they felt not knowing where his mortal remains had been laid.

I didn't know Dries Balkema, but back then I honestly don't think anyone did, even the man he'd worked for. He'd come, I later learned, as I did, on the run from something out East. And he'd worked a year or so for a tough man who broke people the way he broke horses.

I stood at that gravesite and wondered who would remember a man named Dries Balkema. Once those cottonwoods were felled for firewood, who would remember anything? Dust to dust, the Bible says—the whole of the story. After my Rinska's death, I'd come to believe the Bible wasn't wrong about life and dust; the problem with the Bible was that it was itself as spacious as the

31

prairie. It said everything and really, therefore, nothing. I'd come to believe that people put down roots somewhere in its pages because they needed to be assured that in all this wind that is life, some things don't blow away. But once they'd find that place, their faith—their blind trust—would tell them their own version of truth was the only one sanctioned by a Bible they'd come to read only in their own way. Did not God—the Great Mystery, as the Sioux called him—did not God love the Dacohtah and the Dutch? And if he didn't, how could he be God?

Those who'd paid final respects to Dries Balkema had already mounted their horses or climbed into their wagons and left the cottonwoods. Wheel tracks spoked out in all directions from what looked to be something of a hub in the long grass.

I'd not forgotten Mrs. Boon's whispers before the funeral, so once everyone had gone, I followed the Boons' tracks back to their homestead. Arie and his wife and their sons, each wrapped in black coats that seemed two years too small when they'd stood at the gravesite, had seemed genuinely grieved. But no one trusted them. Every tribe has its Arie Boons—Norwegians, Swedes, Sioux, even Dalitha's Congregationals. Burn Boon's wooden shoes, throw a buckskin over him, and paint his half-naked body, make him a full-blood Indian, and people of every tribe and race would still distrust him.

When I got to their house, I wasn't even off my horse before Mrs. Boon stepped out of the front door, holding a sock. She didn't bother with politeness. "I want you to know," she said, "that my husband knows everything I'm going to say. He's in the barn." She turned toward it as if to attest to the fact. "I know what they think. People think he's a monster. You don't know how hard it is to make friends here because of him, but then how can I complain? I've done it myself, I guess. *Ik heb self gedaan.* Besides, say what you want about him, but we can survive another bad year here, even if others can't." She raised a finger, almost as in warning. "Arie is not afraid of work."

Anyone who lived with Arie Boon had a choice—either give in or fight. Mrs. Boon had never given in.

"When I saw you in town—at church—I knew I had to talk to you because Arie and me, we didn't know what to do, really." She rolled the sock up in her hand—it was an old one, mended several times—then put the ball in mine. "There's more to Dries's death than people know," she said, and then she looked quickly at the barn.

"You told me he knows what you're saying," I said.

"That doesn't mean he likes it," she said, then pointed to the sock in my hand. "It's his pay. Dries's. It's what he earned here working for us."

"Pay?" I said.

"There's a girl," she told me. "There's an Indian girl. We've never seen her; she's never been here." She raised both hands in front of her, palms out, like Pontius Pilate might have, then stepped back for a moment and pulled her hands up to her face, almost as if she meant to pray.

"Sometimes he would go to his own church, in Joubert. Anyway, at least that's what he'd tell us. Certainly we'd have done something had we known."

"Certainly," I said.

She looked down at her empty hands. "We didn't know, not until he was dying," she said. "I wasn't there, but Arie says that it was the last thing he said." She tightened her lips as if she might cry. "Arie's a good man, and we've never been in need, but the two of them, they didn't get along." Something in her face told me it was very, very difficult for her to admit what everyone already knew. "He wasn't a boy in years, but in his heart he was a boy." She half-turned toward the barn. "Everything was provocation with him. He never learned to let well enough alone with Arie. In that way, he was a boy—had to have his way. But he was sweet too, I know. All of us—we all have many faces."

"Dries had this Sioux girlfriend?" I said.

"We didn't know," she said. "He was living in sin, right here when he worked for us. This girl, Jan, she told Arie she was with child, his child." She pointed at the sock. "What he told my husband before he died was that all his wages should go to her because she was going to have his baby."

I didn't believe it. I honestly didn't believe it. It would have meant him crossing the Missouri, going onto the Rosebud reservation, finding some girl who wouldn't be scared to death of a white boy, and then—and then getting her pregnant. Impossible.

34

"I didn't know what happened until he came in that morning," she said. "We'd been gone, and the boys were working at De Jong's place. No one was here but Dries, I guess." She pointed out west, past the fence. "Arie found him out there," she said. "He was still alive. Arie saw the tracks around him. Indian ponies. And that's when he said what he did—how he has this girlfriend, and she's *in verwachting,* and how he wants what he's earned to go to her."

"A name?" I said.

"That's all," she told me. "Something else garbled maybe, but that's all."

"Can I talk to Arie?" I said.

"He wanted *me* to tell you," she said. She straightened her apron with both hands. "Maybe you can find this girl of his, of Dries's. But he wanted *me* to tell you."

"I'd like to talk to him—"

"Some things I don't question," she said, shrugging her shoulders. "You learn to choose when to fight."

"He was sure it was Indians?"

"He saw the tracks—Indian ponies."

A door squeaked open in the barn, and Arie Boon stood there just for a moment.

"He didn't have to tell me," she said. She raised her face as if staring into a brutal wind. "He could have kept the money," she said angrily. "He could have decided that out there." She pointed to where she claimed he'd found Dries Balkema. "He had time to simply forget the whole thing. My husband could have kept perfectly quiet

35

about all this, but he didn't." She pointed her finger at me.

She was right. Arie Boon, it seemed, had every reason simply to forget the whole story.

"You think it was hostiles, Sarah?" I said.

Once again, she looked directly into my eyes. "How dare you question me?" she said. "What makes you think they're without sin? Tell me, when you live among Indians like you do, do they seem any more like saints than the Hollanders? Besides, when did you stop believing in your own people? Shame," she said, then turned quickly and walked back into the house.

The sock in my hand was full of coins. I looked back toward the barn. I saw no one, nothing. Those pony tracks would have been erased with the wind that always blows on the prairie.

# ⊰ *Three* ⊱

When I finally returned to our cabin, I was startled to find Dalitha leaning over the table, pointing at a roll of maps unfurled in front of her. She was telling a Sioux friend of ours, Broken Antler, something about Chicago. I was startled in part because I'd just come from Friesland, where a man visiting a woman alone at night would have been out of the question. Dalitha had told me a thousand times that most Sioux didn't think like white men when it came to women; they were, she told me, far more respectful. When all the differences were tallied, she'd say, Indian morality was probably as tight as that of the most righteous Hollander. Yet it seemed to have so little of the fear that erected fences all over.

I'd seen that in her in those three days in which we'd fallen in love, stranded in a blizzard together. I was the one who was squeamish, worried about getting out of the shack where we'd been stranded, made uncomfortable by the fact that the two of us had been so clumsily thrown together by the storm. Of course, Sister Ward—the name the Sioux gave her—did very little fretting at all about anything back then. It was something she'd learned from them—not to be anxious—something they knew even though they'd never been lectured to consider the lilies.

Broken Antler, dressed in shirt and trousers, his hair cut short, was, as people said then, a progressive, someone who'd begun to understand that the traditional Sioux way of life was losing ground to a far greater power, the swarming white culture all around.

"Jan," Dalitha said, startled into the kind of joyous smile that made homecomings a blessing for me, "I was showing him that it's absurd—what the dancers are saying." She spread both hands over the length and breadth of the map, then looked at Broken Antler and laughed, as if to emphasize how crazy the ideas were. "I'm trying to get him to see how impossible it is."

I hung my jacket up on the hook beside the door. "Impossible?"

"What they're saying, these disciples," she said. Once more, she looked down at the map and tried to make it all clear. "Here to here," she said, pointing then raising her hand to Broken Antler with two inches between her thumb and forefinger. "Paha Sapa to here—to the river. Four or five or six sleeps," she said, then looked at me. "To the Black Hills it's several days' travel, right?"

He nodded.

"Now here," she said, looking back down at the map, following some trail to the bottom of Lake Michigan. "Just to Chicago," she told him and raised her hands once again, both of them this time, spread a foot apart. "All white people living here already. Many, many *washechu*. And from here." Once more she drew her hand straight, then passed it over all of the East, all the way to the Atlantic. "All the way to the great waters, many, many, many more—more than buffalo, more than you have ever seen."

Broken Antler studied the map.

"Brother," she said, "it is beyond imagination." She shook her head dramatically. "Those many, many white people—like stars in the sky—those many people will not simply be buried. It will not happen. They won't simply be swept away." Once more she shook her head. "The earth will not be swallowed. Should God eat himself?"

Broken Antler looked up at her, then at me. "Does God lie?" he said.

"No. But his people, sometimes their ears hear songs the Great Mystery is not singing." She motioned to a chair across from them. "This new messiah, Jan," she told me, "he's told them all that in the spring of next year, heaven will come to earth."

We hadn't heard the whole story yet—inklings, yes, but not the whole story.

"Wo-vo-ka," she said, pronouncing each syllable clearly, then nodding at Broken Antler. "A new Jesus, a Paiute, somewhere out West." She shrugged her shoulders. "They've sent some men to listen to him, and those men have returned with a new gospel." She looked at me. "How can I tell him it's all wrong—it's nothing but a beautiful dream? How can I explain that?"

Already in May, the agency people had spoken of this new dance, a strange dance—women and men together, not separate like the other ritual dances. They said they could speak to the old ones, the ancestors—that's what was promised. Keep dancing, and the old ones would arise and speak in beautiful dreams. That much we had heard.

"God will snatch all the *washechu* from the face of the earth." Dalitha drew a circle with her arms. "The earth will swallow them all—all of us."

"Does the president know?" I said.

"Don't joke." She turned back to Broken Antler. "Brother, you must tell your friends—all of them—that what Short Bull says cannot be true. God doesn't lie. But the words we hear in our ears, they are not always the words of the Great Spirit. That you know too."

Broken Antler's eyes never moved.

"It is false hope," she told him. "Like gold that drives the white men crazy. It cannot be true."

He studied every inch of the territory laid out before him, then pressed his lips together, looked at Dalitha, then at me, and pointed himself, west, toward the Rockies and beyond. "If we dance and if we believe in our hearts," he said, "we will see what Wovoka has seen with his eyes. It is promised, if we do as God has commanded."

"Is Wovoka God?" Dalitha said.

"He has seen these things himself, in a vision when the sun stood still."

"And *you* will dance this crazy dance?" she said.

His face showed no expression. "I don't know what I will do," he said and then drew his hands into a clench. "But many will dance." He shook his head. "How can we not believe what Wakan Tanka has told us? We are his people. Sister Ward, how can it be that God would lie to us? Why would he play this joke? Short Bull—he heard the vision from the Paiute messiah. He saw his face. There was no two tongues there."

Dalitha pointed at the map. "All of this land—many, many sleeps wide—all of it, and it is all white people." She shook her head. "Not just me and Jan. Not just the whites in the settlements or on the trains or in the wagons. Many, many, many more. Would Wakan Tanka destroy all of them?"

"He did in a flood," Broken Antler said. "It is told in the book. For their disobedience."

"It is madness," Dalitha said angrily. "Speak to your daughter. Listen to what Anna says. Speak to her if you think I'm wrong."

Broken Antler looked directly at my wife. "Anna is with the dancers," he told her. "She has left the school, and she is already with the dancers."

Dalitha stood quickly. "Your daughter is part of this?"

"She has found a husband. My daughter has left the school and gone to be with him and the dancers."

41

Dalitha put both hands down on the table, and the lamp flickered. "You're sure?"

"She has seen too much of *washechu*," he told her. "The boarding school has taught her evil. She says she knows the white man, inside and out."

Anna Crow had been to boarding school and had returned to the reservation as a teacher. Dalitha disliked boarding schools; they destroyed Sioux families, she said. But when Anna had returned, she'd been a great help in the schools that Dalitha ran.

"Bring Anna here," she said. "Find your daughter and bring her here."

"Am I a white man?" he said. "She has made her choice. She belongs to her husband."

"Bring her here," she snapped. "I don't care. Bring her here anyway."

"Dalitha," I said. She wheeled quickly then looked into my eyes and seemed to awaken. Her hands came up to her face as if she were about to cry, but I knew she wouldn't—not just then. "Promise me, brother," she said more quietly. "Promise me you will tell them all, tell everyone not to do this dance until you have listened to me."

He nodded, and then in the silence that surrounded the people Dalitha had come to love, like a shadow he moved toward the door and left, not looking back.

"Like their stomachs," I said, "their hearts are hungry."

"There is no messiah," Dalitha said angrily.

"What do they know of Bethlehem?" I said. "This man, Short Bull—he found a savior among the Paiutes."

42

She stared down at the maps, then rolled them up slowly and tucked them above the storage box that had become, long ago, her kitchen cabinet. "Anna Crow," she said, shaking her head. Once more, she brought both hands to her face. "I can't believe it. Anna Crow goes with them. If anyone could look through all this madness, it would be Anna. And we'll miss her, Jan. I'll miss her at the school." She shook her head. "Sometimes it makes me want to leave."

I put my arms around her. "You know better," I said. "This is your home." It was good, holding her there in my arms. Coming home to Dalitha in those days, those early days of our marriage—it was always good. "Listen," I told her, "the last mile of the path to this cabin seemed like forever." Because it had.

I can't begin to explain what Dalitha gave me, what she meant to me then, so many years after I'd buried my family. Companionship? Of course. Love? Yes, something I'd thought I'd never know again. But she brought much more into my life. This whole new world of the reservation, for one thing. And passion, plain and simple passion.

While so many found the vast Dakota grassland difficult to love, Dalitha's joy here was a constant delight, even though, on her very first trip into Indian territory, four days in, she'd once wandered from the wagons for a moment to touch a telegraph pole, the only reminder of what she then would have called "civilization." She was just past twenty, and she had to restrain herself from running up and hugging it, she told me.

Back then, she had pledged to give her life to teaching Sioux children, so she'd put down roots on the west side of the Missouri long before you could find a white face most anywhere west of Yankton, save some old French trapper. She'd been here before the buffalo had disappeared, and had come to understand that terrible loss, not just as food but as something sacred to the people among whom she lived. The loss of the buffalo was an open wound to body *and* soul, she'd told me. I was a child of the Book—of the Bible. My father was a Christian leader and one of the strongest believers I'd ever known. That the end of the buffalo was something like the end of God was a fact of reservation life that took me years to understand. But Dalitha was a persistent and passionate teacher.

When Broken Antler had left our cabin that night, we made plans—immediate plans—to try to understand what was going on. We'd heard rumors about this new religion, of course, but when the Ghost Dance came to the Rosebud, it roared in upon us like a fire. Suddenly, it was all over, all around. Dalitha never guessed someone like Broken Antler might be swept away, because when we'd first heard about it, it had all seemed so preposterous, so silly. But our friends weren't silly. Broken Antler was among the most progressive of his people.

So the next morning we left, traveling west farther into the reservation. With the sun behind us, the long, tawny hills stretched out like mounds of golden flax. I remember how any trip across the featureless prairie west of our cabin was still a bountiful treat for Dalitha. That morning she sat beside me, her hat in her hands, the two of us in the wagon she'd driven alone for more than a dozen years at a time when the reservation was far more threatening than adventurous, Crazy Horse still alive, Sitting Bull and his people not only unsettled but hostile.

"You didn't tell me about Friesland," she said. It was early, a whole day had passed since Broken Antler's visit, and we were on our way to Running Elk's encampment. "It was a very sad funeral, I suppose?"

I hadn't told her what I'd learned about Dries Balkema. The night before, it would have been like throwing kerosene on a fire; that's how deeply affected she'd been with the messiah madness. "This Balkema was young," I told her, "and there are some questions about his death. The place is unsettled."

"Because of this?" she said, meaning the dancing.

"Everyone is on edge, about anything."

"Like them," she said, meaning the Sioux. "It won't work, this reservation business," she told me, hooking her hand through my arm. "Lock them all up out here and give them what they need—it won't work. You know that's true."

"I have a good teacher," I said. "But those people back at the Friesland church—they don't."

"Maybe that's your calling."

I told her no one there thought they needed me teaching them anything.

"People learn," she said, pinching my arm. "It might surprise you to know you're not the only man with whom I spent some time during a blizzard."

"Now you tell me," I joked. "After we're married."

"Now that I've got you," she said. "It was the very first winter, and I was out somewhere here." She pointed, as if anywhere would do. "A storm came, but I didn't really know what a storm was, because where I'd come from, there were blizzards but there were always houses and barns." She snuggled into my shoulder a bit, as if she were still cold. "I would've died if it hadn't been for a man, by himself. An Oglala, I think. He happened to find me—my horses wouldn't move anymore in the heavy snow, and I didn't know what to do. For three days he cared for me. I didn't know a word of the Sioux language, and he didn't understand me either, but that was the first time I slept in a buffalo robe."

"You never told me," I said.

"You think you know everything," she teased.

"But you didn't marry him."

"He didn't ask," she said, giggling. "He wasn't a Christian, but he'd done for me what the Bible makes clear is the task of all of us—to love selflessly." She seemed almost to bow before his memory. "Two or three days later it dawned on me that maybe I wasn't exactly the teacher I'd considered myself to be. What was I? Twenty-

46

three maybe. Could have just as well been fourteen. He taught me things I had to learn."

"You were a child," I said.

"I thought I was the vine and they were the branches." She reached for my arm with her other hand and held it. "Maybe that's what you have to teach your people, Jan." Right then, we saw a scurrying herd of antelope moving effortlessly with the motion of the grass. "Sometimes it's not hard to believe what the Sioux do, that everything exists with the breath of God."

I had never doubted her love for me, not since the two of us had been together through our own snowstorm three years before. I knew I wasn't simply something she needed to get along on the reservation; she hadn't even thought of a man herself, she'd told me when first we'd fallen in love. The idea of love and marriage was something a devoted teacher had just as devotedly kept from her mind. It simply wasn't acceptable. Then came our blizzard.

What didn't change was her commitment to those Sioux encampments pitched out over the reservation like drifts of snow here and there on the horizon. As long as we were married, my only rivals for her love would be the people she'd come to serve and the land she'd grown to love.

But there were times when I couldn't reasonably guess how she might react to certain things, and I had no idea what she'd say about the story I'd been told of Dries Balkema. Maybe that's why it took a while for me to tell

47

her what Mrs. Boon had told me. "It seems this boy—this dead boy—wasn't only working on the farm of Arie Boon," I said. "It seems he had a girlfriend. I have money he wanted to get to her—his wages. Mrs. Boon gave it to me. It was what he wanted, what he asked for before he died."

"For a Sioux girl?" she said.

I nodded. I was sure the news was, to her, as unbelievable as it had been to me.

She took her hands off my arm and brought them to her face. "This girl? She must be one of my students."

Boon didn't know a name, I told her, my eyes focused on the path in front of us.

"It can only be that some girl is with child," Dalitha said suddenly. "She must be with child, this girl."

The path we were on was distinguishable only by the hump of fresh grass billowing up from between two parallel depressions. I hadn't even told her about the pregnancy. "Before he died, he told Arie Boon."

She leaned forward, her elbows on her knees, her hands drawn to her face. "And you believe this man?"

I told her his wife had been the one to tell me, and I said I believed her.

"Everyone knows about this?"

"No one."

"Of course," she said. "Does Boon have reason to lie?"

"He could have kept those wages." I held out an empty hand. "I have it. I have what this man left for the girl."

The sun was rich and warm for November, the air deep and heavy, almost as if we were riding beneath the robe of some ancient buffalo. It was one of those few days when there seemed to be no wind at all, just a husky, lingering heat.

For a long time Dalitha sat in silence, the quiet tramping of the horses the only sound in a windless morning air. And then it flowed out. "It must be Anna Crow. Remember what her father said about her finding a husband? It must be Anna Crow." She brought her hands up. Just that quickly, she thought she knew the whole story. "We need to pray, Jan. And then we have to find her. If it's true, we have to find her. It has to be Anna Crow."

Dalitha knew almost every young woman from the bands close to the river, and certainly knew which of those girls might chance being seen with a white boy. And, more importantly, who might want to. In my heart, I knew that if she believed Anna Crow was going to have the baby of Dries Balkema, she was almost certainly right. Besides, Anna Crow had left working at the school for the ghost dancers. Anna, trained in the East in a boarding school—Anna, probably not afraid of white boys—Anna, the daughter of a good, good friend—Anna, with child by a white man, the man who'd been shot.

She held my arm again and stared west down a path that seemed barely visible through the grass. "This man, Balkema," she said. "How well do you know him?"

"Not at all," I told her. "But people say he didn't seem a violent man, not someone who would have done what you're thinking." I knew what kind of story was already being written in her mind. "I'm not defending him."

"And I'm not accusing you," she told me.

"Dalitha, I don't believe this boy would have raped her." Once I said it, the word was out. She didn't respond. I knew she doubted me. "You think you're the only one who can read people?"

"Why did you call him a boy?" she said.

"I didn't mean to."

"You sympathize with him, don't you?"

"He's dead, boy or man. He's dead and in the ground. I'm telling you that everything people say about him makes me think he wouldn't be the type—".

"He forced himself on her, Jan," she said. "Trust me."

"Because he was white and she was Sioux?" I said. "Then why would he make sure someone got her the wages—"

"Guilt," she said. "You and your people are very good at guilt."

"My people?" I said.

"Yes, your people. He knew he was going to die, so he had to make one last leap for eternity. He could close the books on his own life if he made himself clean about what he'd done to some Indian girl, so he told this Boon there was a squaw carrying his child. 'Get her the money,' he said. 'Get this poor girl my money so I can meet my Savior with clean hands and a pure heart.'" She took a deep and audible breath. "That's the story, Jan. I don't care what you say. That's the story."

50

The horse's rear quarters snapped with every step, and the wheels creaked as the wagon rolled clumsily over the rugged path. The morning song of the meadowlark filled the empty spaces in our conversation, and there were many. "It must be a burden to be the only one under heaven who has in her possession the whole of God's truth," I said finally.

"You think I'm wrong?"

"I'm only far less sure that you're right."

"Anna Crow," she said. "The moment her father said it—how she'd found a husband—I didn't even know she was looking. The moment he told me that, I should have guessed there was something more."

In just a few hours we'd made it to Broad Bear's camp, a place that looked emptied. Only a single column of smoke was rising timidly in the windless morning air from one of the several tiny frame houses the Sioux had built since leaving their tipis in the last few years. Broad Bear was aging, but he still owned enough horses to give him some standing. Even though he and his band had lived close to the Missouri River, they weren't among those Sioux to wander into nearby settlers' territory, because Broad Bear was a traditional. He likely thought it demeaning to scratch the soil, to become the farmer the government wanted all Indians to become. To him, planting potatoes was women's work. He was simply an old brave, and he lived the way he saw fit with his two wives, his children and grandchildren, and some in-laws

51

or cousins. His only concession to the changes occurring all around was a frame house in lieu of the traditional tipi.

"It's no wonder no one comes to school," Dalitha said. "There's no one here."

A singularly disturbing cry arose from the shadows around the encampment and continued into a wail. It was something completely new to me back then, a trembling song not unlike a rabbit's terrified scream, like nothing I'd ever heard before coming to the reservation. It was a woman, and the song was some distressed lament that's purpose was obvious no matter what the language. She was singing a death song.

Nothing moved in the encampment. No horses stood or grazed nearby. Even the dogs were gone. In the light breeze, a few ceremonial banners twisted slightly from buckskin-less lodge poles, and what was left of a fire snapped and crackled, tossing out handfuls of sparks. The emptiness all around made the shrill anguish unearthly.

"May you go in there?" I said as Dalitha, without hesitation, stepped out of the wagon.

She looked at me sharply. "Can I not?" she said and turned quickly to walk toward the cabins. An old woman bent her shoulders out of the door, then turned her head slightly. When she recognized Sister Ward, she stepped out and held the door open behind her. I should have known better than to question Dalitha.

Once they disappeared into the cabin, the crying stopped. I stepped down from the wagon and stretched my legs. I was close enough to hear conversation in the Sioux language, close enough to hear my wife's voice deepen to carry sympathy. Sometimes back then, I wondered whether my love for her was little more than admiration for her persistence and dedication, things I had lost. Who could not love her measureless commitment to these people who she had, for better or worse, come to regard as her people?

Soon enough, she stepped back out of the cabin and signaled me in.

It was a woman, and she was young. And there was death. A child. The cause could have been anything—whooping cough or pneumonia. But Dalitha told me, in English, that the young mother claimed the baby had died of fright. Someone had dropped something around the baby, and the child had been startled. And he'd never really recovered. "The truth is, the baby died of hunger," Dalitha told me. "Malnutrition is the cause, and the government is the killer."

She turned back to the mother and asked to hold the child's body. The mother whispered something in her language, and Dalitha took the baby, held it as lovingly as if it had just been born, then held it up to me. Its face was gray, its skin pallid and its eyes closed. "This is what we're doing," Dalitha said. "This is the price of gold. This is what the land costs."

I don't know why, but I opened my arms for this dead baby. Dalitha looked back at the mother and the old lady who was comforting her, and when they nodded, she handed me the child that was no more a child.

Wrapped as it was in blankets, little more than its face was visible, but it was clear that Dalitha's sense wasn't far afield. Its cheekbones had begun to emerge from ashen skin thin as paper. My own children were never starved. I'd held them in just the same way, but they'd looked nothing like this. Even so, I felt the same cursed emptiness from holding what could have been, what should have been. It wasn't the same as it was in Michigan, and yet it was.

"Another funeral," Dalitha said, and I nodded. For a moment, the mother wore Rinska's own gray face. "If you carried that child to your people," Dalitha said, "maybe they would understand."

She was right. Had I lugged this tiny body into that new church in Friesland, maybe people would understand what was happening on the Rosebud and all the new, chopped-up reservations. Maybe if I had said nothing, just passed this child around, arm to arm, maybe then the *washechu* would understand the cost of their new opportunities, their freedom, their dreams.

Dalitha took the child back, then stepped across the dusty floor, gave it back to its mother, and said some things, asked a question—I could hear it in her intonation. The old woman pointed, explained something in subdued tones, and Dalitha thanked her and nodded politely. She reached for the anguished mother, held the woman's arms in her hands, then swept some strands of her hair back behind her ear. There were tears.

Outside, on our way back to the wagon, she said nothing.

"Don't ever wonder why I stay here, Jan Ellerbroek," she said, scolding, once we were on our way. "Don't you dare to ask why after seeing that." She drew a long breath as if to stifle tears.

We were back on the wagon, moving farther west to Butte Creek, when Dalitha said, "She told me the others were with the dancers." She put a hand on my arm. "Is it any wonder they need a savior, Jan?"

## ⊰ *Four* ⊱

E'yaye'ye'! E'yaye'ye!
Mich 'nkshi mita'waye,
Mich 'nkshi mita'waye.

A lone woman in the middle of the dancers was singing mournfully, her head raised in a strange kind of triumph. She was dressed like most of the others in that new, flowing dress—white muslin with billowing sleeves that followed her frantic arm movements in a spiritlike wake, the whole dress marked with moons and morning stars, with handprints and birds, with eagle feathers and long leather fringe.

We were sitting outside the circle of dancers with a half dozen other white people, all of them strangers. I'd been nervous about being there, because our presence seemed a violation of something sacred. But Dalitha had not hesitated, and we weren't the only whites.

"She's seen her baby," Dalitha said, translating. "'It is my own child,' she keeps saying. She says it over and

56

over—'It is my own child.'" She looked at me. "In her vision, she's seen her own child, she's seen her lost baby."

Just a few hours before, I'd held a dead baby in my hands; maybe that was part of the chilling fear that gripped me there at Butte Creek. More than a hundred people were dancing—men and women together—whirling in frantic spins, singing, crying, shrieking in a hundred distinct voices whose pitch and fervor found no place in my soul. I could not help but feel that some white people weren't wrong about the Sioux; some part of them remained not only pagan but demonic.

But I knew better. I had been around the Sioux people long enough to admire them as loving human beings blessed, as are all of us, with their own bit of the glorious image of God. Beneath the buffalo robes, the locks of human scalp, the porcupine quills and eagle feathers, I knew a man like Broad Bear was no more or less a human being than Abraham Brinks. I knew that. In my mind, I'd come to understand it.

But the Ghost Dance struck me deeper—the shrieking, the spinning, the fits of madness, the people dancing into exhaustion and delirium—what I saw and heard and felt went far beyond reason. The staid, methodical beat of the Psalms chanted by a huddled congregation of immigrant believers in some wilderness church was what I'd known as worship. I'd grown up thinking faith was reverence, not madness. The seeming insanity of the Ghost Dance felt not only heathen but almost demonic. I would never have said that to Dalitha, but what I experienced in the presence of the dancers—and it hurts me even yet to confess—made me frightened enough to turn my fear into hate. I could feel it everywhere, and my own reaction made me want to cry.

We had been there since dancers emerged from the sweat lodges arranged in a circle around the tree in the middle of the dance grounds. We'd been there when the holy man called them from the purging steam into the center of the circle, where a tree had been placed, its bark wrapped in plaited rushes, a white flag hanging from its uppermost branch. We'd been there when the dancers, hundreds of them, held hands around the tree and listened to the holy man call on Wakan Tanka, the Great Mystery, the Great Spirit.

Always, Dalitha translated. "We ask your blessing on us . . . give us back our hunting land . . . transport us now to the spirit world . . . bring us back again safely . . . may we see our loved ones . . . hear us, O Great Father."

We'd been there to see the dance begin, a huge circle in half steps, the people moving toward the left. We'd been there when the holy man, from the center of the circle, commanded the dancers to repent of their sins. We'd seen many slash themselves and spread their blood on the tree, some of them even digging out pieces of flesh to show their sorrow. It seemed wrong to watch them try to empty their souls, for that's what they were doing. Powerful men—and their wives—dozens and dozens of them sat before that tree and actually wept in anguish for their sins. I'd never seen anything comparable, even among my own family and church, a strange Dutch people most Americans judged as deeply, even madly religious.

And then the dancers began to wander out of the circle, arms raised, knees high, on and on and on until finally, hours later, some fell to the ground in what seemed sheer exhaustion, thrashing at the earth as if they'd suffered seizures. It took several hours for some of them to spin into fits of exhaustion and fall here and there, others standing over them to be sure they weren't trampled by the dancing still going on around the bloodied tree. One by one, men and women, they spun themselves into what seemed madness. We watched, mostly in silence, as several hundred began to succumb . . . to what? To exhaustion? To burned-out emotions? To visions?

What I saw there among the dancers can neither be described nor explained to someone who never witnessed the ritual. If it weren't for the people's fervor, their earnestness, their selflessness, the whole dance would have seemed to me to be utter madness. Maybe it was.

And then, later, when they appeared to return to this world, each of those dancers claimed to be filled with the spirit of the "other," the world from which they'd come. Each would prophesy about what they'd seen—mostly the very same vision. They'd spoken to the ancestors, they said, and it was beautiful; everything they'd seen and heard was beautiful. Each of them had seen the future, and it was good.

The woman alone in the circle was singing of a child she'd lost. A man stood and told one of the holy men about seeing his father, who, in the voice of an eagle, had told him that the two of them would be reunited. "Another winter," he'd said. Some spoke of seeing the messiah, his bleeding hands and feet, the spear wound in his side. Some described him as a white man who said his own people had broken faith and that he'd decided to abandon them for the Indian. He'd promised the return of the buffalo. No one should fear, because the promises of God were sure. He would give them everything they desired, everything they needed if they would dance, if they would seek his face, if they would abandon the old ways and find their joy in the Lord.

Time and time again, we heard the same sermon—continue to dance, do not hurt others, no more wailing for the dead, trust in me—I am the messiah. We have seen our grandparents, we have seen our lost loved ones, and we have seen the Lord, and he loves us. He wants us for his children. He has promised he will bless us. The buffalo will return, and the white men will be swallowed up when the earth opens. They have abandoned him and given themselves up to their own desires, and now the messiah will bring his love to the red man. We have suffered, and he knows it; he sees our hunger, and he loves us. We have this all—we have seen it with our own eyes. How can you doubt, because the vision has been given to every one of us.

60

"Look at his shirt," Dalitha said to me, pointing at a young man she knew. "He hasn't worn anything that old-fashioned in his whole life."

"Is that good?" I asked.

She covered my hand with hers. "I don't know, but we may as well stop the wind. We may as well stop the sun from rising. Look at them. This morning—you remember, Jan," she said, meaning the dead baby. "This vision— what it promises is so much joy."

"It's a lie," I said, whispering. "It's madness. You said it yourself."

She looked at me sadly. "That from a man who says he doesn't know anymore if God answers prayer." She turned back to the dancers, taking my hand in hers. "Isn't it better to have faith like this than to have none at all? What do these people have? Nothing of what they were and no sense of where they'll be. Can't we at least give them this joy?"

That lone woman dancing in a circle and singing of her dead child stood, her feet only slightly moving beneath her, her face up toward the sun, the sky. There was some-thing angelic about her, something holy. I felt it myself. "But it's a lie," I said.

"How do we know?" she asked. "Do you have a hold on the whole truth of God?"

"No one does," I said.

"Then why not give them this?" she said. "Winter will come soon, and they'll remember their empty stomachs.

Hunger will starve them back to earth. Can't we give them their joy, Jan, give them their peace?"

"Even if it's a lie?" I asked. The young man was singing not far away, others with him.

> Wana'yañ ma'niye,
> Wana'yañ ma'niye.
> Tata'ñka wañ' ma'niye,
> Tata'ñka wañ' ma'niye.
> A'te he'ye lo,
> A'te he'ye lo.

Dalitha pointed. "There is a buffalo bull walking," she said. "They're saying, 'There is a buffalo bull walking, says the Father.'"

We'd been there for more than an hour, and we hadn't seen Anna Crow, perhaps because we weren't looking for her. Once the dancing had begun, the effect of the whole ceremony on both of us was so strong that we'd forgotten about anything else. Before we'd arrived, we knew she had left the school at Wind River Crossing and that somewhere she'd taken up with dancers; that's what her father had told us. But on the Rosebud reservation in the fall of 1890, the dances—and the dancers—were legion. Further west, at Pine Ridge, the hills were full of dancers too. Everywhere you went, people were talking about the spirit dance bringing back the buffalo and the old ones, and swallowing up the endless march of the *washechu*. That day, we hadn't seen Anna Crow, because even at Butte Creek there were hundreds of dancers.

What's more, she'd painted her face red and pulled her blanket up over her head, covering her short hair. When Dalitha finally did see her, she didn't recognize her. Ever since Anna Crow had been to school out East, she'd abandoned traditional dress and hadn't let her hair grow back.

"Behind the man carrying that shield—behind him," she pointed, taking hold of my arm. "That's her," she said. "It's Anna, I'm sure."

All I saw was someone who seemed particularly striking because she'd so luridly painted her face. She was wearing a ghost dance dress, loose and billowy enough to cover any sign of a pregnancy, a girl gone mad it seemed, spinning in the way a child does to create a spell of dizziness. I couldn't see her eyes beneath the hood she'd created with her blanket. Honestly, she was barely recognizable as a human being, much less someone I knew.

Once years and years ago when a friend of mine put a gun in my hand for the first time—I was just a child—I killed a muskrat caught in a trap. It was the first time I'd ever killed any living thing. That animal's death dance, spinning madly as if it could chase away the pain, was a memory that has always stuck with me. And that's what I saw once again when I watched that hooded young woman spin wildly then fall to the ground.

Dalitha got to her feet and walked directly into the circle of dancers. For a moment I thought I should go too, but Sister Ward, known among most of those dancing, had a reputation for strength and wisdom. She wasn't one of the holy men in black skirts, the revered Catholic priests, but nearly everyone there recognized her the moment she stepped out of the cover of the bushes where we'd been sitting.

Anna was lying in the dust, someone over her to protect her from being stepped on. The man—it was an old man, a medicine man, I think—looked down at her for a moment, then listened as Dalitha told him something. Grudgingly, he stepped back.

What she did then surprised me, even though it shouldn't have. I would have expected her to speak harshly to Anna, but she didn't. She knelt at the girl's side, pushed the blanket back from her face, and, with her fingers, rubbed gently from the bottom of her cheeks to the edges of her jaw. I don't believe she said anything.

"Nobody back home would believe this," a man next to me said.

The coat and tie, even the hat on his head, made it very clear he was from somewhere back East.

"I don't know that I believe it myself," the man said. "That your wife? That woman who just marched out there?"

I nodded.

"Either plucky or plain stupid," he said.

Instantly, I hated him. I looked away toward Dalitha, who was stooped over Anna Crow, one hand on her shoulder, the other still gently touching her face.

"Who are you?" the man said.

"Name is Ellerbroek," I told him.

"Norse or what?"

"Dutch."

"What in God's name you doing out here?"

"We live here," I said. "The two of us."

"Settlers?"

Dalitha was trying to get Anna to her feet. Something in me distrusted the man, and I refused to look at him.

"What do you know about this madness? I work for a newspaper—several in fact," he said, and he pulled out a little tablet and wet his pencil with one quick swipe across his tongue. "They goin' on the warpath? That's what people are saying. People are saying that this whole dance business is only a warm-up for a fight."

Dalitha had Anna sitting up, upright and smiling. She was smiling. She wasn't saying a thing—Dalitha was doing all the talking—but at least she was partially up.

"She knows them, doesn't she, your wife does?" the man said. "Name's Parker, Frederick Parker," he said. "And you are?"

"Ellerbroek. I told you," I said.

He was watching Dalitha. "I got to hand it to her. Looks to me like she's doing what she can to save some lost souls."

I simply hated him.

"She's a missionary, isn't that right, I bet," he said. "Nobody else stupid enough to want to live out here. Even the soddies are crazy, if you ask me. But it's a story all right, isn't it? People back East love it. It's all Buffalo Bill to them. They eat this stuff up. What'd you say your name was?"

I looked him in the eyes for the first time. "Ellerbroek," I said again, and when the man reached out a hand, I started to stand in order to avoid it.

"Listen, you need some money sometime, I pay good for stories, you know?" He didn't seem at all surprised that I wouldn't shake his hand. "If you know something about what's going on with these people—you know, from the inside—I pay good money." He slapped my sleeve with the back of his hand. "We can all use a little extra, right? Especially here, although I don't know where you'd spend it. Ain't a thing to spend it on out here anyway."

Dalitha looked over at me, full of concern. Anna Crow simply smiled.

"Usually I'm hanging around the agency somewhere," Parker said. "I mean, if you got something people'd like to read, you can just about always find me."

"Why should I tell you anything?"

"Put it this way. If people like you don't, I'll just make it up." He pointed to the madness going on in front of us. "It's a funny thing about people; most of 'em'll believe most anything if they want to." He winked. "White buffalo—sure. The earth swallows all the settlers—you bet. The dead walk again—I'll put my money on that one, sure thing. Same thing with people back East. They'd believe anything they want to." He looked up at me. "You look

66

like a smart enough guy. You know what I'm talking about."

"This is their religion," I told him.

Parker tossed a hand. "They're all nuts, and you know it." We watched as Dalitha stood and started walking back toward us. "I got to get something out of that woman of yours," he said. "Think she'll talk to me?"

I figured I had to get rid of him. "You know the Lord?"

"I can fake anything."

"You're wrong about that," I told him. "She'll read you like a book."

"A holy book," Parker said, giggling.

"You see her walk into the middle of all of that dancing?" I asked. "You see my wife do that?"

"I told you she was gutsy," he said.

"Trust me, Parker. You don't want to talk to her right now. Just trust me."

He shoved his little pad back in the pocket of his fancy coat.

It was the first time I'd ever spoken to a man from the press, and I hated him because he didn't care about anything other than his precious story—not about truth, not about Dalitha or Anna Crow, not a bit about the Sioux.

Maybe I'm making too much of all this. Maybe I'm telling you all of this too slowly. But what you want me to tell you cannot be written with just a swipe of my tongue on the stub of a pencil. What you want to know makes me reach back as if I could hold the whole reser-

67

vation in my own hands, because there are stories here that Parker never saw and never heard—and you must.

"We have to speak to her," Dalitha said when she came back. She spoke as if Parker wasn't even there. "We have to speak to her somehow, Jan," she said again. "Not in the middle of this either. That's not what I mean. We have to talk to her. I'm not leaving until we do."

But both of us had had enough. We'd been there already for several hours, I believe, before we'd seen Anna Crow. We knew very well that the dancing could go on almost indefinitely, until all of them had dropped from sheer exhaustion. I can't say that we ever really felt in danger as we sat there and watched what was going on. None of the dancers seemed at all concerned about the fact that white people were observing; what they were doing was their passion, their faith. They were worshipping.

When night came, however, we became a bit apprehensive about staying too close to the dancers. When darkness fell, fear came up in both of us, so powerless we felt in the drums, the shrieking, the wailing of prophecy. After seeing Anna out there dancing, Dalitha was committed to staying around to speak to her, but we got in the wagon and went east to set up our own camp, the sound of the drums rolling over the open spaces between us like distant thunder.

Even though Dalitha had been living on the Rosebud for fifteen years and knew hundreds of Sioux men and women, one characteristic of the people she'd grown to love but never quite absorbed was their almost unremitting silence. Not that she jabbered or carried on end-lessly, but when I came into her life, I became, unwittingly but joyfully, that someone she'd missed speaking to for more than a dozen years.

That night, however, she said very little. Even though the weather that November seemed nearly perfect, the days warm and slow to depart, on that particular night dusk settled in chillingly, as if to remind us that winter was coming at long last. Dalitha clung to my arm as our wagon bumped and rolled across the prairie.

"What scared me more than anything," she said, "was the peace in her eyes."

"You've never seen it before?"

"Framingham," she said, "the boarding school. If Marcus had known what kind of anguish he caused out here with these children's families, I don't think he would have taken them. Maybe I'm wrong. I don't know."

"Framingham?" I said.

"The boarding school won her soul, just the way Marcus claimed it would, because the moment she set foot back here on the Rosebud, she knew home wasn't the same. She knew home wasn't home anymore."

"She told you that?"

Dalitha shook her head. "I only see it now. I was happy, you know—it seemed to me that we'd secured the heart of one of them for our cause. She would be a teacher in the schools."

"And now you think she has peace?" I said.

"It's the peace she thinks she has that scares me."

69

I had always assumed my wife's distaste for the Framingham Indian Boarding School, way out East in Massachusetts, had come, at least in part, from the fact that Marcus, the man who ran the place with only the best of intentions, took away some of her own best students.

"They become trophies, these children," she said. "The Framingham band plays all over the East. 'Come and see the savages,' the advertising says, I'm sure. 'Come and see the pretty little children of the vermin who massacred Custer. Watch them toot their horns.'" All the while she was holding my arm. "They are trophies. Anna was a trophy," she said. "Maybe to me she was a trophy too when she returned—a trophy, my trophy. And now what scares me more than anything is her peace, peace like a river."

We stopped at a stand of cottonwoods in a hollow. "Right now, maybe it's a blessing, this peace of hers," I said.

She turned her face into my arm, and I believe she cried, although she didn't want me to know. "How many times will we have to change her, how many times will we have to break her like a pony, before she will be what we want her to be, Jan? All of us, Marcus and now us too? How often can we break them before something in them dies?"

That's what she said, I remember.

During the three years I'd been married and living on the reservation, and during those years before that when I'd driven countless wagons across its rolling hills, I'd never felt as deeply *washechu* as I had when I stood out-side that circle of frenzied dancers, paralyzed and seem-ingly so far away. Even Dalitha felt it, I believe.

It wasn't much later when a single rider appeared on the bluff above the hollow where we sat eating some pro-visions we'd packed. Dusk had lingered, and the sky was clearing to the west, so it didn't take long for us to rec-ognize Broken Antler, Anna Crow's father.

When he got to our fire, he dismounted, tied his horse to a tree, then came and sat beside us. He took some of the bread Dalitha offered and ate slowly, as if there were nothing on his mind. All of that had to be done before he would say anything. I'd lived with the Sioux long enough to understand. When finally he did speak, there was no small talk.

"In my heart, a wound is bleeding, Sister," he said.

The fire popped and crackled. I finished my bread and wrapped it back up in the bag. The coffee was strong. I poured a cup for him, offered it, and he took it.

"It was not good to send her away to that school," he told us. "I should have listened to the voices of my fathers, because they said she would never come back."

"She's here," Dalitha reassured him.

"But she is not my daughter."

The night was getting cold. Dalitha was wrapped in her blanket and I in mine as we sat beneath a sky that still glowed from a departed western sun. Broken Antler sat beside us, his own blanket only half raised toward his shoulders. He wore no ghost shirt; he wore instead white man's clothing beneath his blanket. His hair, although long, was unbraided and undecorated. He had not been among the dancers.

"You asked me to believe in Jesus, Sister," he said. "You said he had come to take away our sins and carry us to glory." His fingers, I remember, were folded, as if he were in prayer. "It is not just a story white people tell their little ones, you said, but a story that is true for the Great Father in Washington just like me, like American Horse, like Sitting Bull, like the Oglalas and the Santees and the Hunkpapas and the Brule—even the Pawnee. It is a story for our people and yours, you told me." He brought his hands up before his face, still folded, then opened them and looked into his palms. He closed them again and stared at Dalitha. "I believed you."

"And the angels rejoice," Dalitha said quietly, but loud enough for him to hear.

"My daughter too once believed," he said, "my daughter who was for three winters far away in a city of white people. And now my daughter says this Jesus has come again, to us, because we are poor and suffering and because *washechu* put him on a cross to die. 'He is here,' she tells me, 'and now he loves us.'" And then he stared. "Why should I not believe my own child?"

Dalitha did not wait. "Why don't you?"

He looked away as if slapped. "How can one vision be true and the other not?" he said. He spoke down, as if talking to the earth. "Why should I believe you and not

72

my own daughter? Because we are Sioux and you are *washechu?"* he said. "This Jesus came to you, you say. Does he so hate the people that he would not come to us?"

"Let us pray to this Jesus," Dalitha said, and she did. Right then, she asked the Lord to come into our hearts and make the darkness disappear so we could see the light of the morning. She asked for a blessing on Broken Antler and his daughter, Anna Crow, and for all the people whom he loved.

The whole time, Broken Antler stared into the fire.

"You need to bring her here," Dalitha said when she finished. She pointed at him, at me, and back toward the camp. "You and Anna Crow and Jan Ellerbroek and I—we need to talk."

"She is not a child," Broken Antler said.

"All the more reason," she told him. She raised one finger. "Just this one time, Broken Antler. You promise her that Sister Ward says we need to speak to her just this one time, and then we will leave her to her will."

"She will not come," he said.

"You are her father."

He put his hands down on the ground, lifted himself to his feet, walked to the tree where his horse was tied, and unwrapped the reins.

And that's when we saw her standing there outside the reach of our fire. She appeared to have found us on her own, and she stood alone, the red paint on her face now gone. She had come in silence, still in the dress of the dancers. She'd walked into our camp out of the darkness of the night. She had come to us.

What tore my heart was the way she acted toward her father, not with anger or malice or resentment, but with love. She didn't address him directly with her eyes—that wasn't the Sioux way of giving respect. But a few quick glances and the deliberate selflessness showed him her love.

I don't know why, but when I saw her there, her hair still cut short from Framingham but her face dark and round and so very Sioux, I couldn't help but see what might have been had my own Jantje, my daughter, lived. For a moment I forgot the dancing in some unasked-for vision of what never was. For a moment I could have cried, so much I coveted. The guilelessness in the smile she gave her father made me believe that Broken Antler was, in the words of the psalmist, still highly blessed.

Dalitha stood. She hadn't when Broken Antler had come, but she stood now and waited—I know she did— for some cue by which to greet Anna. I know she wanted to hold the girl in her arms. Dalitha had loved unceasingly for all her years on the reservation, but the Sioux people were no more profligate with their affections than were my own. Perhaps it was because in their hearts they always held Dalitha higher than she had herself—the white woman who had given them so much was beyond their touch. Whatever the reason, I knew Dalitha well enough to understand that she waited, trembling, for some indication that she could hold Anna Crow.

And I don't know what it was, but somehow she saw that it would be right, because otherwise she would not have gone to Anna Crow as she did just then. Something was between them that neither Anna's father nor I could read, something created in her perhaps by her experience at Framingham. I don't know the mysteries. But somehow Anna Crow signaled that it would be acceptable to embrace. So they did.

Soon enough, they parted, holding each other's hands. Dalitha led her back to the fire, then pointed toward her father and nodded, asking him too to sit. Dalitha looked at me, and I gave Anna my cup, then poured it half full of coffee. Anna took four or five sips, glanced back and forth from her father to Dalitha, her eyes occasionally lighting on me.

Broken Antler never once touched his daughter, simply sat beside her at the fire. That was enough. It was clear he was more than happy that she'd come.

Her face was round, as I remember, soft and fleshy in a way that wasn't thin and angular like so many of the truly beautiful Sioux women. Which is not to say she wasn't pretty—some women, white and red, carry remarkable beauty even if their features are not chiseled and perfect; and that night Anna Crow seemed beautiful, perhaps because of the warm smile she wore so effortlessly. She was clothed in the dress of the Ghost Dance, a dress fashioned of unbleached muslin, a rim of blue painted around the neck, symbols—birds, stars—imprinted across her chest, heavily fringed, probably made just a few days before.

But Dalitha wasn't wrong. The young woman I'd seen not that many hours before, writhing in the fog of dust that rose above the circle of dancers, that young woman seemed almost incapable of carrying all the joy that tipped from her soul now.

"It is our religion they won't let us practice," she said finally.

Dalitha shook her head as if she didn't understand.

"You know the army is coming," Anna said. "You've heard that?"

We hadn't, neither of us.

"The army comes to stop the dancing," she said. "White people came to this country so they could believe what they wanted, so they could worship. The *washechu* traveled from beyond the ocean because they wanted to worship their own God, and now bluecoats come to stop us from worshipping him."

Neither of us knew about the bluecoats, but that they would come wasn't hard to believe. Settlers all around the reservation were scared to death.

"They will try to stop you?" Dalitha said.

"For what other reason would the Great White Father send so many?" she said. She knew the word *president*, I'm sure, but she deliberately chose to use reservation language.

"There are many bluecoats?" Dalitha asked.

"From every direction, and we have done nothing. You tell me one thing we have done. We have done nothing but dance, as Wovoka has told us. Because there will come a time, Sister," she said, and her arm rose and her finger moved quickly into a point, "there will come a time when the dust will cover the earth once again, and the messiah will come. He has heard our suffering, and we will not be swallowed."

One could describe Anna's eyes as vacant, her mind devoted to a dream grown from misery and desolation; but what was there in her face was assurance, the deep confidence that all things would work together for the good of those who were loved.

"Is this what you learned at school?" Dalitha said.

I remembered what Dalitha had said about breaking this woman, as if she were a pony, over and over again.

"What I learned at school," Anna said, "is to be white. What I know now," she took hold of her face lightly, then pointed, "is that I am red."

"Is this God you worship red?" Dalitha said.

She shook her head. "He is your God, but he loves us and not you because he has heard our cries of pain. You will see."

"And me, Anna?" my wife said. "And me and Jan here? Because we are white, we will die?"

Without dropping her eyes, she chose not to answer.

"How do you know these things?" Dalitha asked. "How do you know these voices are true voices, that they come from God Almighty?"

77

"In my heart I know, just like you." She pointed at both of us. "How do we know what we believe?" She tugged a bit at the shirt she was wearing. "We know it here, and I know it here, Sister Ward."

Three years it had been since Dalitha and I had spent three days in a blizzard. For three of those years, we'd been married, and in all that time, I don't believe I'd ever seen my wife's face so heavy with sadness.

Anna reached for her father's hand, something I thought then and still think today was very much non-Indian. I think he was as surprised as we were to see what she had done. "When I returned from the *washechu* school," she said, "my grandmother's house, it was hard to be inside when I came back because I thought it was too dirty. What I felt in my heart was that I could not live in my own grandmother's house, and I cried and cried, and that night I stretched my hair—I pulled it down and down because I wanted it to grow long again."

We were sitting together, Dalitha and I. She shoved her fingers beneath my leg.

"If they kill us," Anna said, "we will die with honor." And then she smiled. "We will die for our faith." She nodded at her father. "What you told me when I left for school—always be brave, always be good, my daughter. You remember?"

He remembered, he said.

"We will not make a fight," Anna Crow said. "You tell me, Sister Ward, when was it in all of this that the Indian made war? Never. You want our buffalo, and you take our

78

buffalo. You take them all. You want our land, and you take whatever it is you think you need. And now you want our souls. But there are things we won't let you take. The bluecoats may kill us all, but we will die Indian. The old ones say, 'Tomorrow is a good day to die.'"

And that's when, suddenly, all three of us noticed we weren't alone. The man had come in silence, as Anna had, but it seemed clear somehow that even though he'd purposefully not joined in, he'd been listening to the entire conversation. He stood just inside the circle of light, no blanket, no leggings, no feathers, nothing to distinguish him as being Sioux but his long hair and a beadwork vest.

If Anna Crow had searched quickly for a husband and a father for her child, she hadn't simply taken the first available man. That's what I thought, anyway. This man— none of us knew his name then—looked very strong. If you think he looked angry, you will be as surprised as I was, not only at his unexpected appearance—as if suddenly he had decided we should know he was listening— but also at the mercy in his eyes. He didn't look at us. He looked only at Anna Crow.

"This is Wolves in Camp," she said, introducing him. She didn't refer to him as her husband.

I looked at Dalitha, who smiled and nodded politely.

Anna said something to him in the Sioux language—I think it was that he could sit with us—but he shook his head.

The moment I laid eyes on him, I thought I would like him, even though he chose to stand outside the circle but close enough to be seen, as if he wanted to make clear that he was standing guard.

"He's from Butte Creek?" Dalitha asked.

"Standing Rock," Anna said.

I knew only that Standing Rock was a few days' travel north and, after the west-river land had been broken up into different areas in 1888, a whole different reservation.

Dalitha did not let his presence stop her from questioning the girl. "And how does Wolves in Camp feel about tomorrow being a good day to die, Anna?" she said, pointing.

"It is as she said," Wolves in Camp told her.

We'd both assumed the man didn't know English. "I'm sorry," Dalitha told him, nodding.

"I was for one winter at Framingham," he said.

"One winter?" Dalitha asked.

"My father came for a visit and took me home."

"You are a dancer?" she said.

The way he glanced at Anna, just for a moment, made me suspect they weren't in full agreement. I didn't know whether or not Dalitha had seen that look. What she did see, I'm sure, was his eventual nodding assent. But I'd seen hesitation, and that's why I said what I did. "Wolves in Camp, will you also dance from now till spring, every day?"

"It is our faith," Anna Crow said. "It is what we believe, and you have no right to take away our faith. America is a land of freedom, Marcus said. 'In America, people believe what they want,'" she said, mimicking his voice. "We believe in the dance."

"Wolves in Camp?" I said again.

This time he didn't hesitate. "It is as Anna Crow says."

"But is it what God says?" Dalitha asked.

There was no smile on Anna's face, but that unmistakable conviction that had scared Dalitha was painfully obvious. "God tells us to dance. I myself have seen the vision. It will come to be, I am sure. The buffalo will return." She looked at her father as if to convince him. "The buffalo will return, and it will be as it was. He has seen our suffering, and he will come to save us. We believe what the messiah has promised."

"Anna Crow," Dalitha said, as if there were, in fact, a bridle in her hands, "what if all of this—all of these visions and all of this prophecy—what if it turns to dust?"

"You should wish it so," Anna Crow said.

"And what of your children?" Dalitha asked. "If this is a dream, what of your children?"

"How can you ask me to deny the words in my heart?" she said. "You are no different than bluecoats, Sister Ward. You see? All of you," and she pointed at me too, "all of you want us to be like you, and we won't be you, because we can't."

"So you will dance?" I said.

"We will dance."

"And what of your children?" Dalitha said. She was trying to nudge Dries Balkema's confession into this conversation, a confession I'd almost forgotten.

But Anna Crow's perfect faith ran like a river's spring current. "Our children will be raised in Indian ways," she said, and once again she looked at her father and reached for his hand, something Broken Antler, I believe, found difficult to understand. She simply wanted him to believe.

"Surely you don't think Marcus and all those people in Philadelphia and New York—you've been there, Anna—surely you don't believe they all will die."

"It is as Wakan Tanka has said, and Wovoka."

"How can you know?"

"Because it is in my heart too," she pleaded. "Because I have seen in a vision that the old ones will return." She smiled once again at her father. "I have seen it is true. With my own eyes, I have seen." And then she said something that surprised me greatly. "And you, Sister Ward—what is it that you believe?"

I don't think Dalitha guessed Anna would have, or *could* have, turned her own question on her.

"I don't believe the buffalo will return in the spring," my wife said, "and I don't believe the earth will open up and swallow all white people. I think it is something the people would like to believe, so they do—not because in their hearts it is good for them, any of them."

"You have told me what it is that you do *not* believe, Sister Ward," Anna said. "Now tell me what it is you do."

I don't know that she could have asked Dalitha a tougher question. I could feel the anger building in my wife as she sat beside me, anger that grows from a soul that is somehow penned like an animal. "I believe in God," she said assertively, and then I added the words of the creed: "The Father Almighty, maker of heaven and earth."

"As do I," Anna said.

"And in Jesus Christ, his only begotten son, our Lord," I said. And once again she nodded. "Who was born of the virgin Mary, suffered under Pontius Pilate, was crucified, dead, and buried, he descended into hell."

Anna Crow looked at me and smiled like someone who has taken a bellyful of pounding and begs for more.

"The third day, he rose again," I recited, "ascended into heaven, and sitteth at the right hand of God the Father almighty; from thence he shall come to judge the living and the dead."

"He's not here," Dalitha said. "He's not out West with the Paiutes, and he's not at Standing Rock or Pine Ridge—he's at the right hand of God."

"And where is God?" Anna said.

"In heaven," Dalitha retorted.

"He is here," Anna said. "And I hear his voice in the song of the lark and cry of the rabbit. He is in the wind, and he speaks, and I have heard. Have you heard the voice of God, Sister Ward?"

I don't remember ever seeing my strong, strong wife so disarmed. In part, she was frustrated, I'm sure, unaccustomed to getting nowhere with someone like Anna; but I knew she had no ready answer about hearing God's voice. And Dalitha wasn't about to lie. It was anger, I think, that drove her to do what she did. She answered by getting to her feet and walking to the wagon behind us.

"We have some money for you," she said. "From a man in the settlement east of the Mud—east of the Missouri—someone who must have known you, perhaps." All of this she spoke with her back to us, not as if accusing. "He gave it to a man and told him that it should come to you, this money," she said, still not looking at her. "You knew him maybe. His name was what, Jan?"

"Dries Balkema, from across the river," I said.

Dalitha thought the only way to win this moment was to play the big card, even though she was playing in the presence of Anna's father and the man I imagined to be her husband. It was an act of desperation, and I wasn't proud of her.

I hadn't taken that purse along, so she dug some coins out of her bag then pressed them in a handkerchief and tied them in a knot. She came back to the fire, stood beside Anna, and offered the bundle. "He said he wanted you to have this—his final wages."

Nothing—not a hint of emotion—appeared on Anna's face as she took the handkerchief, and if she hadn't left, if she hadn't gotten to her feet at that very moment, signaled her father good-bye, nodded toward Wolves in Camp and then toward us, I think I would have believed that Dries Balkema or Arie Boon or even Arie's wife—that one or all of them had lied.

Not another word was spoken after Anna Crow took that money from Dalitha's hands. Not another word.

Her father left quickly behind her. He was the only one who showed any emotion, and it looked to me as if it were anger, directed at us.

# ※ Five ※

That we would head east the next morning, back toward the river, seemed impossible after everything that had happened. It was Sunday, neither of us had any responsibilities, and nothing had been settled. Other than Anna's abrupt departure, we had no clear sign of what Dries Balkema reportedly had confessed with his dying breath. Anna's faith had served only to make Dalitha more determined to get her away from the madness of the dancers. So we went west.

From Butte Creek to the camp of Two Stones wasn't all that great a trek, and we knew Rev. Thornburgh would be holding services in the little church on a bluff above the Little White River. That morning, we awoke to crisp, cold air already beginning to warm in the heat of an unnaturally temperate sun. It was November, late November, and I don't recall any fall being so long and warm as the fall of 1890, the autumn of the messiah craze.

86

The memory of Dalitha standing over Anna Crow as Anna awoke from her vision, out of her trance, out of whatever it was she'd fallen into, was the picture that kept appearing to me. "Does it worry you that she's pregnant—the dancing?" I asked Dalitha as we made our way across the prairie. "I just now thought of it," I said. "The dancing, it could be dangerous for the baby."

"Maybe there is no child, Jan," Dalitha said. "Maybe there never was. Maybe there was and is no more."

"What do you believe?"

"When I hugged her, I wanted to know," she said. "But I couldn't tell. Touching like that, it's not the Sioux way, of course—not with me, anyway. I couldn't hold her that close."

"He would know—Wolves in Camp," I said.

"Something tells me no one does. Something tells me if she is carrying a child today, she is carrying it very much alone. We have to get her out of there."

The Reverend Thornburgh's little church would disappoint most white people; it was nothing but four walls with tree stumps for chairs. But on a good Sunday, the crowd could number sixty or seventy. That morning only five of us were there—Thornburgh himself, an old Sioux woman, her grandchild, and the two of us. The sermon—I don't remember a word of it—was barely audible above the drums and singing from the camp close by.

In the years that have passed since that Sunday morning, I have never sung "Nearer, Still Nearer" without remembering that place and that time, because the drums, carrying like wind across the open prairie, the drums and the eerie keening served to mock the words of that old hymn. "Nearer, still nearer/Close to thy heart," we sang, even though what we heard and where we were and the things that had happened since we'd gone after Anna Crow seemed to make me think I was never farther away.

Maybe it was the drumming that prompted Dalitha to do what she did once we left the church—the drums and what had happened around our fire the night before. She said nothing of her plans to me or to the preacher, although she spoke courteously to him, even intimately, the two of them sharing their fears about the whole situation. But then, almost coldly, she told me she had to go to Two Stones's camp, to the dance, because there were things she had to say. There were things that had to be said. I didn't ask what, not that my question would have mattered.

Ten minutes it took for us to walk to the cabin of Two Stones, the chief of the band. A number of women stood around outside the cabin as if waiting for something.

"I must talk with Two Stones," Dalitha said in the Sioux language. Behind us were the piercing cries of the purging ceremony, the bloody requests for forgiveness.

A young woman threw back her blanket and ran in, then returned quickly, leaving the door open.

Dalitha didn't pause for a moment when she got inside. She bowed slightly to Two Stones, nodded a greeting to the two or three others with him, and then spoke. "You do not believe all this, my friend," she told him. "This is madness that both you and I know about. You don't really think that in a few months the old ones will return. Right now, while we are standing here, you are deceiving your people by letting them dance. You are deceiving them, Two Stones, because in your heart no voices say that all the old ones will return." She pointed west. "You and I— we have seen the buffalo vanish. They will not return in twenty sleeps. They will not return even in the Moon of the Red Grass Returning. And worse, some of them believe that *we* will all be gone," she pointed to me and to herself, "that *we* will die like ants swallowed up by the Great Father. You are deceiving them, all of them."

Two Stones took the pipe, puffed, then passed it along. Had Dalitha not been a woman, he would have offered it to her. He was a large man, imposing—even while seated he commanded attention. His jacket was old and hung with hair locks from ancient battles; his war bonnet lay at his side, an old cavalry cap on his head. When finally he spoke, it was just one line, intended to end the conversation. "I cannot stop them," he said, and then he reached for the paint, dipped his fingers in the bowl, and started to color his face.

Dalitha stormed out, and I followed her. We walked directly to the dusty plume that already hung above the wide circle of dancers, but I stayed behind when she kept right on going into the very center, where finally she stopped at the foot of the sacred tree, oddly enough—

and I'll never forget this—the one hung with an American flag.

"Brothers and sisters," she said. "You know me. I am Sister Ward from the Mud River, and I have taught your children. I have lived among you for many winters. Together we have eaten buffalo. Many of you have prayed with me."

In a minute, there was silence. She waited. Even the drums stopped.

"You, Louis," she said, pointing at a man whose face was blue, "you know better." She pointed at women. "Many Fields, Tired Horses, Calves Jumping the Water—you are all my friends. I know you all. Your hearts are pure and right. You do not speak in twisted tongues."

She'd stopped the dance's every movement.

"For you I have always had an open heart. I have not spoken in lies," Dalitha told them, using everything she had in her without raising her voice. "And now I am come to say that you all know better than this. You, Jacob," she said, pointing at a man already on the ground. "Get up," she said.

No one moved.

"You are not deceived by this. Inside, Jacob, you know that all of this is not the truth." She looked at the man on the ground, an older man, his war bonnet slightly askew on his head, his shirt already thick with dust from where he'd been kicking in the dirt.

"In your heart, you know that when the sweet plums are ripe, Sister Ward and her new husband will still be here. You know that," she said. "I am myself *washechu*—this you know—as is my husband. So right now, before all of us, I call on the Great Mysterious to take me and take him, to rip us from the circle right now, at this moment, if he will."

There she stood beside the tree at the very heart of their faith, her arms raised.

"Make good on your promise, Great Mysterious," she said, addressing their god, her head raised defiantly. "Take me now and my husband or show your people, here and now, that all of this is no more true than the shining waters that always lie beyond us on the grass." She held her hands out beside her, offered both of us, her eyes closed and her face raised.

Nothing moved. Near the camps, dogs barked. The song of the meadowlark ran in the air like some unseen golden thread, something forgotten but suddenly once again heard. All around, the dancers stared into the sky, awaiting some bolt of lightning, some trumpet, some rifle shots—anything.

Then, right in front of her, the man she called Jacob swept the dust off his sleeves, pulled himself to his knees, placed a hand on the ground, and got his feet beneath him. He looked around at a hundred dancers, removed his bonnet, slapped the dust from the feathers, replaced it on his head, and started walking away.

Many followed that day, many of those who had come to dance at Two Stones's camp. Many of them walked back to their cabins or tipis, many got on their ponies and rode away.

But not all.

For a time at least, the strength that Anna Crow's faith had drained from Dalitha the night before returned with this triumph. Like Elijah, she'd stood there among the dancers, begging Baal to strike her dead; but there was no thunder, no lightning, no whirlwind, and when so many of the dancers simply began to leave, so did we, in a kind of reverent silence, neither of us speaking a word until we were far out of earshot of the dancers.

Good weather on the Rosebud can seem a blessing. Heat can stifle breath, cold is a killer; in July, thunderstorms roam like wolves in packs. But that morning as we made our way back to the Butte camp, the sky's beauty was a picture of something eternal. Beneath it, the dusky prairie lay peacefully; the world, for a moment at least, seemed a glorious Sabbath.

Dalitha wouldn't want me to tell you that as soon as we'd come far enough away from the camp where she'd begged a deaf god to kill us both, she cried—not loud, not hunched over on the wagon, not audibly at all, but she cried. Her hands were folded, and I believe those tears were a part of a prayer. I know she didn't want me to talk to her, even though I'm confident she wanted me to know of the tears. For a half hour, perhaps, she sat beside me, and neither of us spoke. Silence is something

you learn in the presence of so much sky and so much
land.

"Someday, maybe," she said later, "we'll live out here,
you and I, and I'll keep chickens, and you'll farm the land,
and maybe we'll have children."

"On the reservation?" I said.

Once again she took my arm. "Do you think I could live
somewhere else?"

What she'd said wasn't meant as a question. She
couldn't live elsewhere, of course, and neither could I
after those years. Sometimes people wondered how it
was we fell in love—the two of us, both near forty, so very
different in a way. But there were times in those years
when, for me, the thought of Dalitha living out there alone
for all those years without me seemed impossible, just
as impossible as my being without her. We loved because
we needed each other, I think. We fell in love in three
snowbound days, in a blizzard I think God smiled into
being.

The camp at Butte Creek was deserted when we
arrived, and many of the tipis were gone. Smoke from last
night's fires rose gently in the windless air, the flags and
ribbons from the Spirit Dance tree perfectly motionless,
brush arbors still standing. There was no Anna Crow.
There was no Broken Antler. There was no Wolves in
Camp. There was no one. It was as if some great force
had simply swept them off the earth.

So we followed them by way of the path they'd left in the matted prairie grasses. In a few quick lessons, we'd learned enough about the messiah craze to know there would be no school anywhere right then. There was no doubt my work was stacking up, but I wasn't the only teamster who operated on the edges of the reservation. I was sure my friends at Valentine and Rosebud Landing—my friends all over the region—would be happy to take up the extra business. Dalitha and I hadn't packed provisions for more than a day or two, but if we made our way to Rosebud Agency, we could resupply. So we kept moving, west and south, believing we would find Anna Crow somewhere between the Little White River and the Pine Ridge reservation.

The farther we went, the more unfamiliar the country became. Even though Dalitha had lived on the reservation for a long while, she knew fewer and fewer of the Sioux who lived beyond Butte Creek. Every camp we visited wore the same sad livery of poverty and starvation; even the dogs were skin and bones from the driest summer anyone could remember. No meat hung in the sun, and the camps themselves were nearly deserted—a few old women maybe, here and there an old man among them. When we asked, they all answered in the same way—the dance, the Spirit Dance.

At some point before we came to the agency, we saw a smeared tan cloud at the horizon and knew immediately what it had to be. So we left the road and followed no path at all through the heavy brown grass, the wagon

94

jumping and rolling beneath us. We knew we had to make our way toward that flat smudge of dirt in the sky.

When we arrived, two things were remarkable about this group—the sheer size, sometimes hundreds of dancers, and the number of observing whites. Some had driven up from Nebraska after hearing reports about the craze. They were there in buggies—men and women from as far south as Valentine, some dressed up as if they were on a holiday outing. Otherwise, what we saw didn't seem unusual anymore. It seemed this Wovoka from somewhere out West had made very clear what kind of dance was supposed to be undertaken, and here—as at Butte Creek and Two Stones's Camp—the rules were followed religiously.

There were no cabins, even though most of the Rosebud Sioux had by that time moved out of their tipis and into framed structures. Here there was nothing but tipis, as if the whole reservation had taken a trip into the past. The tipis stretched out along the bank of a creek for almost a half mile, and for more than an hour, with the drums beating excitedly behind us, we searched for Anna Crow. By the time we arrived, there were dozens of dancers in the dust—"dying," they called it, and to me their vision experience seemed something of death itself. We sat outside the circle and looked closely to see if we could find Anna Crow, but we couldn't.

Dalitha knew several of the participants. When she could, she asked them if they had seen Anna or Broken Antler. None of them had.

I kept watching the dancers while Dalitha walked through the encampment, tipi by tipi, searching but finding nothing, no sign of her, no trace. No one had seen her, but neither did we see anyone we recognized from that first dance at Butte Creek, the one that had been the smallest of the dances we'd seen.

"Hey, it's the Hollander," someone said, and I turned into the face of Frederick Parker, the newspaper reporter. He slapped me on the back as if we'd been friends. "So what do you know about an Indian named Short Bull?" he asked.

I shook my head.

"I figure your wife probably knows him," he said. "He's one of the ringleaders, and he's from back East somewhere." He looked around, kept looking around at the dancers, at the observers, at everyone, as if somewhere there was a better story. "She here?"

I nodded.

"Seems a bunch of them went out West to meet this man, this Wovoka. You know the story?"

I shook my head as if I didn't.

"Short Bull was one of them—and all I got is that he's got a head full of steam because he saw Jesus Christ in war paint in Nevada," he said. "You get what I'm saying? Anyway, I got to get a line on him somehow, you know. You think that wife of yours knows him?"

I had no desire to play his game. "He's from Rosebud?" I asked.

"He was one of those who went all the way out there to get this information, you know—on the redskin that saw the very first vision—that's Wovoka. Some people call him Jack Wilson."

"Don't know," I told him.

"Don't know what?" he asked.

"I don't know if my wife knows some Brule Sioux named Short Bull," I said, as if I were talking to him from across a room.

"She's a fanatic too, huh?" the man said. "I mean, yesterday you told me she wouldn't talk to me unless I knew the Lord."

I'd forgotten. "That's right," I said.

"Tell you what. You ask her about Short Bull, and you get anything, you let me know. I pay good, cold cash for help." He narrowed his eyes and smiled. "This thing is building," he said, a half smile on his lips. "You watch, wooden shoes. Ain't going to be long and the air's going to get a little sticky for the likes of us."

"What do you know?" I said.

He looked around. The keening of the dancers made it difficult for us to hear. "There's white people who can't take this without seeing the devil, and good Christian people ain't going to stand his dancing up a storm around here. You know what I mean. You learn anything and you let me know, all right?"

That was the second time I'd seen him, the second time he'd offered me money, and the second time I never said a word about him to Dalitha.

We hadn't found Anna Crow. With the knifelike sounds of yet another Ghost Dance behind us, we headed for the Rosebud agency.

In those early days on the reservation, there were no settler towns to speak of anywhere, except the agency. You might assume that coming over the hills as we did that next day, riding into a community of white people— the *only* community of white people for miles around— would have brought us great relief. But it didn't.

Throughout the years so much of what Dalitha stood for, so much of her work on the Rosebud drew her into unceasing conflict with agency authorities. I made my living both before and after our marriage by hauling salt bacon, green coffee, all kinds of foodstuffs, not to mention building materials, silver for the cash annuities, and, often enough, people out to Rosebud, but the agency itself often left an unsavory taste in my mouth. The place was a necessary evil, but inside its walls it seemed there was always a shortage of wisdom and too much money, a dangerous mix. Fine people lived there, to be sure. But so did scoundrels, and politics made it very difficult at times to determine who was who.

Rosebud Agency was a collection of frame buildings, homes and offices, and a few huge storehouses, encircled by a twelve-foot stockade designed to keep out the people the place was intended to serve. Maybe forty or fifty tipis and ramshackle dwellings were thrown up just outside its walls, home to what almost everyone disparagingly called "Agency Indians" or "Hang-around-the-forts," those who'd sold their souls, some would say, for crumbs from the white man's table. Just north of the agency stood the sprawling store of Rosebud's licensed trader, a lucrative business just outside the gates. Come ration day, every Sioux family in the area left the agency with something to trade, and the white trader usually made out like a bandit.

This time when we drove in, however, it was clear that what Anna Crow had said was right—everywhere you looked there were bluecoats. The growing military presence on the Rosebud reservation was something I'd never seen before—and wouldn't again, ever. The agency was fully armed, military units setting up everywhere.

It was intimidating, even for us, to be surrounded by so much cavalry. Both of us had been to Rosebud Agency so often that we knew almost everyone inside. But now it seemed that everywhere we looked, military people had planted themselves, as if this were their world now—which, in fact, it was. Around the whole place they were building excavating trenches, like they were expecting some kind of grand assault.

Dalitha went directly to the office of the agent, and I went to the warehouse, thinking there might be a telegram for me, offering some work.

Scotty Devans wore a sprawling mustache whose ragged ends spread out like twin clumps of ragweed beneath his chin. He swore like a sailor, drank like one too, but he never lied to me. He had a habit of deliberately speaking in a bad Swedish accent whenever I came

in, even though I'd told him a thousand times I was Dutch.
I don't believe he ever knew the difference.

"Out and about, Sven?" he said when I came in that day.

"Don't know how else to make a living," I told him.

"So tell me, after all those years of single life," he said
with a wink, "that woman of yours—that missionary—
she's hungry, I bet."

"Think the worst, Scotty, if it brings you some joy. But
you tell me, those troops out there, digging—that's not
for exercise, I take it."

He leaned over the desk. "You want my opinion—if
McGillicuddy was still at Pine Ridge and not that lily-liver
Royer, no one would be dancing." He slapped the counter.
"Or if they were, none of us would care. We got a lily-liver
out here now, and he's shaking in his boots. But he don't
know a thing. And listen to this," he said, leaning back.
"I don't like the whole annuity business—never have,
never will. But if you promise people something, then
you blame well better deliver."

"They're getting shortchanged?" I said.

"The Indians are dying. You must have seen."

I'm ashamed to admit that I'd almost forgotten holding that dead baby.

"The buffalo are gone," he said, "but sometimes I think
they've all just moved to Washington." He rolled his eyes
and pointed at his temple. "But then, who am I to blacken
the reputation of that good and noble beast?" He turned
around behind him. "Got some things here for you, one
from your family."

Two notes from Valentine about some fares that needed delivery, and another, postmarked only "Ellerbroek." My father must have wired a number of places he thought I could have been.

"On my way to Dakota," it said. "Arrive early December. Church business. Hope to see you. Rev. Pieter Ellerbroek."

I had no idea what would draw him to Dakota, except me perhaps, his second son, the prodigal.

"If someone's dead, I don't want to know," Devans said as I was reading.

"My father's coming," I told him, although I suspect he knew as much already.

"May the saints be with you—and with him. And with all of us," he said. "It's dang good for business, of course, all these Eastern boys around here, but it's also downright stupid, if you ask me."

"You're not scared, I suppose."

"I'm always scared out here, but this is an ordinance just waiting to go off. Our only hope is winter," he told me, twirling the ends of that bushy mustache. He reached for the bottle he kept under the desk. "A good blizzard will cool everything down here. Ever try to dance in a blizzard?"

"My people don't dance," I said, winking.

It was peculiar, I thought. My father was coming west to Dakota.

The agent was gone, but the people in his office told Dalitha that, by latest reports, the dancers were moving farther and farther away from the agencies because there was some fear among the settlers—and from this man, Royer—that real danger was building.

What was unmistakable to everybody was the greater military presence, something every last Sioux couldn't help but notice. The president himself had made the military responsible for order on the reservations, Dalitha said. That's what she had heard in the agent's office. To her, that was not good news.

"I want to keep going," she told me when we were back aboard the wagon and just outside the stockade. She nodded west, farther into more dangerous territory. "We have to find Anna." She looked at me. "But I won't go alone."

A month ago, she wouldn't have paused for a moment; she'd have sent me back east to Rosebud Landing. But the fear I'd heard in Scotty Devans's voice, I heard in hers too.

"'Whither thou goest,'" I said.

"This is not your job."

"I'm a teamster," I told her. "This is my calling."

She took a deep breath. "You should have married a nice, plump Dutch girl back in Friesland," she said.

"What makes you think Dutch girls are plump?" I told her. "They're beautiful, every one of them."

And so we left, west again, over land that rolled more than it did on the Rosebud, but land that seemed just as empty—almost fearfully empty. There was too much going on all over the prairie west of the river, and to ride for hours the way we did and see no one seemed some-how wrong.

Only rarely had I done much work on the Pine Ridge reservation, which was served through the railroad at Rushville, not Valentine. Pine Ridge was the reservation of the Oglalas, not the Brules; and the land, closer to Paha Sapa, held more hills and gullies. Here and there, long stands of pine ran along the prairie's hide like lengthened shadows, ridges of darkness that gave the Black Hills their name. Back then it was the land of Red Cloud, at one time a terror to the government, but a skillful chief who'd learned, better than most, how to deal with white people.

Dalitha told me how the agent was attempting to con-tact what leaders he could, trying to talk some sense into them. Washington had ordered the agents of all four reservations to create a list of troublemakers. "Everyone is worried," she told me. We were moving west along the White River. I had no idea where exactly we might cross the line into Pine Ridge, only that it was some miles beyond the spot where the river elbowed west.

"My father is coming to the settlement," I told her, as much to change the subject as anything. "There was a wire there. I'm surprised he could have guessed where I might have been. He's coming in soon, and he wants to see me."

"Bring him here," she said. "We should, you know—we should bring everyone we can out here. Maybe they'd understand." She shook her head. "I'm sorry," she told me. "It's all I can think about, I guess. Your father—what is it he wants to do here?"

I didn't know. I told her I couldn't imagine that he'd entertain a call to one of the churches in the settlement—he was simply too much the theologian for this kind of frontier. The only trails he ever wanted to blaze were the new ones he thought to discover in the old words of the Scripture.

"Maybe he just wants to see you," she said.

And that's when they appeared. There were six, and what I remember best about them is that they were dressed for battle, something I really hadn't seen before—around ceremonial campfires maybe, but not out there in the open. They must have been watching us for a while, and it never dawned on me or Dalitha to be on the lookout. I don't know that she'd ever been accosted that way before.

They rode hard out of the string of trees above us, Winchesters in their hands, feathers streaming from bonnets and buckskin. Their painted faces, their battle cries—I will never forget.

When I reached beneath the seat for the rifle, Dalitha grabbed my arm. Instead, she pulled a handkerchief out of her dress and waved it, pulling me up in the seat so that both of us were standing, making far better targets, I thought.

They didn't fire a shot, but they rolled in with a cloud of dust, their ponies prancing and jumping, as full of spit and fire as the riders seemed to be themselves. They were young, maybe eighteen or so, maybe a bit older. Their leader was wearing a fancy vest that looked like something only an older warrior could claim. Two of them had military-style hats; all of them toted rifles.

The one in the vest pushed his Winchester at us, a sort of roundhouse swing that was meant to say in a very general way that he'd use it if need be. "Money," he said, and just like that he was off his pony. The others pointed their rifles. My hands went up.

When Dalitha reached for her bag, one of them shot in the air.

"They think you're armed," I told her.

One of the men with the military hats shot again. They didn't want us saying a thing they didn't understand. With his rifle, the one in the vest motioned for Dalitha to go ahead and pull out her bag, which she did. He signaled for her to throw it down to the ground.

The one in the vest quickly gave another the reins of his pony, then retrieved the bag and ran through it quickly, tossing out the contents like so much trash, looking for silver.

I felt a rifle in my back. No words were spoken—we were supposed to understand what they wanted, and we did. Slowly, I reached in my coat for my wallet. I got pushed—the barrel made me lurch forward, and I nearly fell from the wagon. I raised my hands again as if to signal that there was no other way for them to get my wallet than for me to reach for it. A gentler nudge told me to go on.

There was more money in that purse than I care to remember. Not long before we'd left, I'd been paid for a job and carried the money with me. I shouldn't have been carrying all that cash, but I was. The moment I took it from my pocket, I assumed it was gone. If that was all that happened, I told myself, I'd be happy.

Slowly, carefully this time, with my left hand still raised, I reached into my coat, drew out the wallet, then tossed it to one of them, the one with a blue forehead and twin suns painted beneath the fringe on his shirt. The man in the vest whooped when he finally found Dalitha's money, and the blue forehead did the same when he found what I'd had. He held up a fistful like a prize. For a moment, the others crowded around as if it were a spectacle.

"Wovoka says to treat everyone fairly," Dalitha said in the Sioux tongue. "The Paiute messiah, he says to harm no one. He says to love all peoples."

Four of them remained on their ponies, but the two who were standing beside the wagon looked at each other, shocked that this white woman could speak their language. Some words passed between them.

"He says if you do not do as he says, the buffalo will not return and the white people will not be swallowed up in the dust."

"Wovoka," the man in the vest said.

"The Paiute," Dalitha said. "Jack Wilson—the messiah."

He stuck her money in the pocket of his vest, then tossed back her bag, emptied, the rest of its contents strewn at his feet.

106

"How is it you speak our tongue?" he said.

We were standing, both of us, hands in the air.

"For many winters I have lived beside the river that is muddy," she told him, gesturing back toward the east. "My name is Sister Ward. For many winters I have been a teacher here."

The men looked at each other. The one with the blue forehead riffled through my wallet and took everything, stuffed it all into the pocket of his shirt, even my father's note.

"What do young braves need so badly that they must shoot and steal to get it?" she said, not as an accusation.

"Guns," the vested one said. "Guns and bullets."

"The Crows?" she asked.

For a long time, the one in the vest studied Dalitha's face. He even stepped closer to the wagon, the rifle still in his hand. Then he looked at me.

"Your husband has no tongue?" he said to Dalitha.

"He does not know your language."

"He is a Christian?" he said—the one word I understood.

"Yes," she told him, "he is a Christian. His father is a great minister. He preaches to many white people."

One of the men on the ponies said something almost inaudible. The man in the vest looked down at the lump in his pocket from the money he'd taken, banged it once or twice, then nodded toward the one who'd pilfered my wallet. That man smiled, as if to say they'd done just fine.

"Wovoka is a man of peace," Dalitha told him. "You know that. Not once did he say to buy guns and kill whites. You know what he has said."

The one in the vest took the reins of his pony from the one who'd been holding them. He swung himself up and over that mount as only a young man can, then turned just slightly back to us. "Wovoka," he said, "is many sleeps away." He raised his rifle, never really took aim, but raised it, pointed, then shot and screamed the kind of triumph chant that chilled even Dalitha, who'd heard most every Indian song. The one with the blue forehead shoved his rifle into my back.

"He wants your coat," Dalitha said.

I pulled out my arms and grabbed it by the neck, then threw it to him. Immediately he put it on and showed it to the others, who laughed and told him, I suppose, how handsome it was. One of them pulled his pony up to the back of the wagon and jumped off, then tore through our belongings, probably hoping there was something there—there wasn't. But then he spotted the rifle and let out a shriek, grabbed it, and knocked me down—for no reason, really. He threw down my rifle to one of his friends, then hit me with a glancing blow that crumpled me in the wagon. For a moment, everything swam around, even though I didn't pass out. Pain flashed from the front of my head into my ear.

Dalitha stooped beside me and put her hands on my head. I told her I was okay. I could see her, and I had this dim sense of what was going on. "Don't push them," I said. "Maybe they have what they want."

And then one of them said something, yelled it derisively. I don't know what it was exactly, because Dalitha would never tell me. But it made her very angry.

"Warriors don't count coup on enemy without weapons," she said angrily, and in a moment, the one in the vest—he was on his horse—rode beside the wagon and stuck his barrel in my face, looking straight into Dalitha's eyes.

This is what she told him: "When the earth swallows w*ashechu*, your eyes too will be dimmed. You're no better."

He looked at her, then at me—judging, very clearly, what he'd heard. Then he swung his eyes back toward Dalitha and laid a stare on her that was meant—I swear it—to drop her to her knees, a stare that lasted a long time, uncomfortably long for a young Sioux warrior. When she didn't drop her eyes, when she held up against it, he slowly backed off, pulled down that rifle, then sat for a moment right in front of us on his pony and screamed some victory chant. Then he smiled, as if it had been a pleasure to meet his match.

In a moment they were gone.

Would he have shot me if Dalitha hadn't said what she did, hadn't backed down one bit? I don't know. She had often told me that some good Christian virtues were almost useless on the reservation. If Christ were a tiger and not a lamb, she used to say, more Sioux would have found him interesting. To this day, I believe that when

Dalitha cursed that man by associating him with *washechu*, when she wouldn't back down from his piercing eyes, it was respect for her that saved my life.

Highway robbery was unlike the Sioux people, but early winter, 1890, was no ordinary time on the reservation. What's more, it wasn't unusual for the chiefs of all those bands spread out across the prairie to have trouble controlling their young braves. And traditionally, one became a man only by way of violence.

"Are you okay?" she said when they were gone, her hands up around my face.

Were we lucky to be alive? I don't know. We would not have been the only whites to die during the messiah craze, but for those young men to murder us in what amounted to nothing more than a simple robbery—in other words, without real provocation—would have been unusual. But then, young men geared up for battle can sometimes be less concerned with who it is they fight than just that they do. It matters little their race or religion.

We turned back east. The hunt for Anna Crow would have to wait.

## Six

There comes a point when courage and indomitable will begin to look like stupidity or, even worse, madness. My aching head told me that it was time to rethink what we were doing, but I didn't have to say it to Dalitha. She understood just as clearly as I did that as long as we had no real idea of where Anna Crow might be, going farther and farther west into the Pine Ridge reservation was as dangerous as it was futile. Without much discussion, we turned back east.

For some time, we replayed every minute of the attack, as if describing it to someone who hadn't been there. I told Dalitha I'd been afraid of the one in the vest because he had too much at stake on how he did his job—he was obviously the leader, and we were nothing more than the means by which he'd build his reputation. Dalitha shook her head. They were just rowdies, she said, and they wouldn't have shot us. They were sporting.

"Sporting?" I said, rubbing the back of my head.

"Not *sporting* either," she said, "but now that it's over, it's something they can sing about. 'How we took the money from the *washechu* in a wagon.' Maybe it will get them wives. That's all they want."

"You weren't scared?" I asked.

She looked at me strangely. "To the bone," she said.

"Really? I didn't think so."

She giggled. She honestly giggled. "It is so much like you to ask a question like that—'Were you scared?'" She pushed at me with her shoulder. "How could I not be scared? Of course, I was. But that's not the answer you're after."

I told her it was a simple question.

"There are no simple questions with you," she told me. "It's something you inherited from your father, I think. What you want me to do is tell you every last thing that went through my mind and heart because it's all got to make sense somehow." She squared an imaginary chunk of something with both her hands. "Everything has to make sense in your way of doing things, Jan. Everything has to fit. You want to weigh it all up; you want to understand. I know. I've seen how you Hollanders talk together."

"And you don't, I suppose?" I said, playing along.

"You people like to think, Jan," she said. "I simply act."

"You people?"

"The Hollanders who call themselves Calvinists," she said. "There's nothing you like better than to think and discuss what God Almighty wants." She raised her hand

and flapped her fingers like a duck. "Talk, talk, talk—get all the *T*s crossed."

I don't mind saying that she got my goat. "So how do you know what you do is being done in the name of the Lord if you don't think about it?" I asked her.

"Because he's in me," she said. "Because he's in my heart."

"You think you're God?" I said.

"You know better," she said. "I know that I'm doing what God wants me to do."

"You and Anna Crow."

"There," she said, "you're doing it again. You know what you're doing? You're doing what you always do, always trying to think things all the way through to some resolution. You know what it is, Jan, this thinking things through—with you people, it's sporting. That's exactly what it is, it's sporting."

"At least you don't have a sore head," I told her.

She took off my hat and ran her fingers over the bruise. "Don't be so sure."

Dalitha was right. I knew she had been afraid. And I think I also knew why she could act so fiercely at Two Stones's camp and during the attack. She was far more sure of righteousness than I was back then, far more sure that she was doing the Lord's work.

In an hour or so, three bluecoats rode up. From the moment they descended the ridge, we saw they were military, and even though they weren't riding fast, soon enough the braids whipping from beneath their hats made it clear they were Sioux. I thought they were scouts; Dalitha said reservation police. This time I was right.

In fact, I knew one of them—Frank Price, a mixed blood with a coat sleeve full of stripes, who, when I first started work as a teamster, sometimes hung around Valentine looking for work. When I told him we had been searching for a girl named Anna Crow, he said he'd never heard of her. He pointed at the butte behind them. They'd been beyond that point when they'd heard the shots, he said. They sounded as if they were close. They wanted to know what the attackers looked like and in which direction they went. "You have no guns?" he said.

I told him they'd taken my rifle.

"You can't tell me that the people want some kind of war," Dalitha said. "I won't believe it."

Frank Price looked at her strangely. "Miss Ward," he said, "I'm sorry to say this, but I don't know if they want to fight so much as it seems maybe some of them just want to die." Then he turned and looked up to the ridge. "Just beyond that butte," he said, pointing, "is Company B—Sgt. Marley. We're under orders to bring in anyone we see."

The patrol Frank Price took us to was doing reconnaissance. Marley, the sergeant in charge, was white—that was the way the army did things. I say that because the Ninth Cavalry was Negro, buffalo soldiers, an outfit with a reputation for being the toughest fighters in the army. When I think about it now, the fact that buffalo soldiers were there on the Rosebud raised all kinds of fear among the Sioux, because when braves spotted them on their horses, they probably thought the army was getting ready to kill them all.

Marley, a man in his late forties, as strong and as tall as any of the men under his command, was one of those who, even when they get old, never lose an ounce of muscle. He was happy to see us, maybe because our simply being out and about on the reservation made him think the situation wasn't as dangerous as everyone else thought it was. He'd been reading a newspaper. He pointed to it after we introduced ourselves. "Four men killed," he said, "not two hours from here. You hear any of that?"

I told him I hadn't. It was obvious he didn't know who Dalitha was, because he spoke only to me, as if she were a squaw.

"Read the Omaha paper lately?" he asked.

I'd never read an American newspaper before I'd met Dalitha. "What's it say?" I asked.

"You'd think we were all going to die. Was a time, I think, when newspapermen took their jobs seriously, never reported rumors." He slapped the paper against his sleeve. "The greater part of this," he said, pointing to the paper, "is likely hearsay. Or worse."

"Worse?" I said.

He looked up at me, surprised, I guess, that I hadn't understood. "How long you live here?"

"Not long." I pointed at my wife. "Dalitha's been here for fifteen years."

"You two married?" he said, an accusation.

I nodded.

"Believers, I bet, aren't you?"

"Sure enough," I said.

"She a missionary?"

"After a fashion," I told him. I lied, but he seemed like the kind of man who would love that answer.

For the first time, he looked at her. Then, embarrassed, he lifted his cap. "I guess I should have known the only civilians crazy enough to be out here right now would be those who love the Lord." He offered his hand, and she took it, and everything changed. "Satan's got an outpost around every corner," he said. "The world's a forbidding place. I'm thankful I'm just a-passin' through."

"Aren't we all?" Dalitha said, playing along.

"The older you get, the more you see of it—sin, I mean," he said. It seemed almost difficult for him to say what he did in front of Dalitha, as if the hint of something vile would singe the halo he'd suddenly created above the head of such a fine Christian woman. "People around here, you know—along the Niobrara and all over—all they want is more people." He looked up, as if to know whether he could go on. Then he pointed. "It's good business to have the army here. We need provisions and such, so the merchants make good money. Besides, with us here, more settlers'll come—that's what they figure. That's good for business too."

"If there was gold at Pine Ridge," Dalitha said, "we'd push 'em all out, wouldn't we?"

"You get what I'm saying," he said. He picked up the newspaper, folded it, slapped it against his hand. "Satan's like a spider, I think—making this web for all of us." He shook his head. "There's good people out here, but the smell of money, it turns 'em all into coyotes, I think. Isn't that what the Lord said himself? 'It's the root of all evil is what it is.' Isn't that what he said? You folks know, you're believers." Then he stood and exhaled, as if he could, with a good deep breath, blow out sin. He looked around at his troops as if they were children. "They're good folks, the coloreds. I work with 'em every day, and I swear by 'em too." He put his hat back on his head. "And whole lot of 'em just love the Lord," he said, and then he turned back to Dalitha. "I respect you, ma'am. I respect what you been doing out here, because the harvest is plentiful and the laborers, I just bet they're few and far between."

We rode back to the Rosebud agency that day, a cordon of Negro soldiers surrounding us, with Marley going on and on about sin and righteousness and the Holy Ghost. Dalitha threw in an amen now and again to hold up our end of the conversation.

But what he said early on was something I never forgot. Even though I'd worked for Valentine merchants for several years by that time, I'd never stopped to think about what it was Marley had explained, that the army—

all those bluecoats digging in at the Rosebud agency—
was downright good for business.

News moved quickly on the reservation at that time;
in some ways, the place was more up-to-date than you'd
think—the telegraph kept everybody in touch with some-
body someplace else, and the army claimed even Sitting
Bull and Kicking Bear's people read newspapers so they
could keep track of what was going on in their own back-
yards. Besides, the Rosebud reservation was itself little
more than a thinly stretched small town with clusters of
neighborhoods in camps, each presided over by a band
leader. The news got around in those camps quickly, men
roving daily from one part of the reservation to another.
With the buffalo gone and intertribal warfare outlawed,
there was little for them to do but hunt when and where
they could, race horses, wager a little, and wander from
camp to camp.

When we returned to the Rosebud agency, it was clear
that things had changed. Scotty Devans told me he'd sent
his family to Valentine, as had most of the other white
workers at the agency. He wasn't proud of that, but with
the army in charge, he told me, people didn't ask questions—they followed orders. I'd gone to his office to pick
up some provisions, including another rifle. My credit
was good with him.

"Don't start to think you're leavin' this place—you and
Miss Ward," he told me when I was looking through
telegrams. "You might think you are, but you're not. The

brass ain't lettin' anybody pull out of here now. They're scared they'll pick you off the prairie with a bush of arrows in your chest."

"It's not that bad," I told him. "We got bushwhacked ourselves yesterday."

"The truth?" he said.

I pointed at the bump on my head. "Wasn't a war party," I told him. "I was scared, but it was just kids."

He shook his head. "If you ask me, the army is creating this mess. Some of them," he said, looking around for eavesdroppers, "some of them live by the old 'good Indian's a dead Indian' thing. They're spoiling for the kind of fun they ain't had since the old days." He slapped the counter angrily, something he had a habit of doing. "Not all of them, either; I'm not saying that. But the ones in charge—and that goes all the way back to Washington— the way their names get the headlines is fighting, you know. No different than the Indians. But winter'll end the dancing. You just watch."

But winter didn't come.

Hundreds of soldiers were bivouacked around the agency—cavalry, infantry, and more than a few Hotchkiss guns. We'd returned on a ration day, and it brought in the Sioux from all over the reservation for the goods the government would distribute. Inside or outside the stockade, the air—and it was still warm, still balmy, even though it was late November—was more prickly. You'd think twice about lighting a pipe.

119

Back then, most places on the reservation you could walk all day and likely not bump into another human being. People accustomed to that kind of elbow space don't breathe easily when everywhere they look they see people, many of whom they don't like. I knew Dalitha couldn't take that compression, even though she was born and reared back East. When I left Scotty, I wasn't looking forward to meeting her, because I assumed she'd heard the same thing about our being stuck at the agency and she'd be fuming. Then we'd leave anyway—that's what I thought. And I was right.

A man named Stanton, the agency saddler, I think, had been out and about on the reservation the day before, and as soon as he could gather a crowd inside the compound that morning, he told his tale, how he'd seen the dancing himself yesterday, how the Sioux were all painted hideously and almost stark naked. An exaggeration, I'm sure.

Stanton had to shave his eyelids in order to see out of a thick beard he wore like a vast red bush. He was standing on the boardwalk, his hat in his constantly moving hands. "And then they made me look right there into the sun," he said to a dozen men standing around him. "They pointed," he said, and he swung around, looking for the sun, then aimed directly overhead. "'See there!' they said. 'See there! The Indian messiah is coming. See him there.'"

Half the men stared up at the sun themselves at that moment.

120

Then he dropped the hand he'd been using as a visor. "I was scared like unto death," he said, "so what was I supposed to tell them but, 'Sure, I'd seen him, sure I did, up there stepping right out of the sun.'" He looked around at the crowd. "Boys," he said, "them Indians just loved that. They thought that was wonderful that I saw their lord."

Men giggled. There were no women around.

"And then I hightailed it back," he said. "I got every last bit I could out of that horse and thanked the Lord I still had a scalp."

That newspaperman, Parker, was copying down every word.

I walked out to the gate, thinking maybe I'd see some of my friends—draymen—but it was likely I was a day late, because they would have come in yesterday with all the annuities for ration day. The Sioux—men and women— were lugging provisions toward their horses outside the stockade. Most of them used travois back then, even though it hadn't been that long since some brilliant thinker back East figured the Sioux should all have wagons now that they were farmers. So Washington sent them a couple hundred wagons, even though not more than a half dozen Sioux had ever driven one. White traders made a mint, exchanging those perfectly good wagons for whatever it was the people really wanted—most of the time guns and ammunition.

Maybe a quarter mile outside the stockade wall, just south of the agency trader's place, a whole crowd of Sioux were listening to someone who looked like he was preaching. Not that far away, dirt was flying off the shovels soldiers were using to dig trenches. In lines so straight they could have been drawn with a ruler, canvas army tents stood almost everywhere.

I remembered then that Parker had been looking for some information about Short Bull, one of the men the whole council of Sioux had sent to Nevada more than a year before to meet with the Paiute messiah, Wovoka. And there he was, dressed ceremonially, a fancy porcupine quill vest hanging over his chest, feathers swooping off the left side of his head and what looked to be a gold medallion hanging around his neck—one of those the Washington bureaucrats loved to give Indians who paid them a visit at the capital. Some hair locks dangled across his shoulders.

It was noon, I think, and the only other white man standing there was Scotty Devans, who'd just left work for lunch. I walked over beside him, and he translated.

"There may be soldiers around you," he told his people, "but pay no attention to them. Continue to dance." It seemed to be a lesson in worship. He had everyone's attention. "If the soldiers surround you four deep, three of you upon whom I have put my holy shirts will sing a song I have taught you."

I don't care what color, some people have a pure gift to hold others' attention, and so it was with Short Bull. His sharp, sharp eyes were piercing, and his face seemed sculpted from flint, his lips flat, almost nonexistent. I

122

don't think he ever raised his voice. He wasn't tall and he wasn't stout, but he knew how to use his eyes when he spoke. I shouldn't make him a charlatan, because he wasn't—he didn't "use his eyes." He believed what he said, and what he said right then was something that scared me deeply.

"And when the three of them in holy shirts sing the song I have taught them, some soldiers will drop dead."

Hundreds of soldiers surrounded them at that very moment.

"The rest will run, but their horses will sink into the earth. The riders will jump, but they will sink into the earth and you can do what you desire."

I don't know that there can be anything more fearful than blind faith.

"Now," he said, "you must know this, that all of the soldiers and the white race will be dead. There will be only five thousand of them living on the earth."

Short Bull was a disciple of the messiah. Every man and woman who heard him speak there—almost within earshot of the troops digging trenches—every man or woman knew he was one of the few who touched the hem of Wovoka's garment. He was dressed in animal skins; had he been eating locusts and wild honey, he couldn't have been more a prophet. And the people listened closely, their eyes attuned, the way my father would have liked his people to attend to his preaching.

Short Bull finished everything he wanted to say, it seemed, then looked around and saw me and Scotty

Devans, the only whites. The others turned, and I realized that even though everywhere around the agency there were bluecoats, neither Short Bull nor his congregation wanted us in their sanctuary.

We walked away in different directions.

Crowds of Sioux were moving in and out of the gate and milling around the sloping hill that slowly stretched up toward the gates of the agency. Most were packing provisions and trading away some of the annuities the government had just given them, the goods they'd been promised for land that had once been theirs. Ghost shirts and robes were everywhere, but I didn't recognize a single person just then.

It was time for me to find Dalitha and tell her we would likely be detained, if she didn't know it already. From what I'd just heard from the mouth of the holy man, Short Bull, maybe our staying at the Rosebud agency for the time being was for the best—that's what I was thinking.

I hadn't moved far up the path toward the stockade when a hand came down hard on my shoulder from the back. My first reaction was fear, maybe because I'd just felt Short Bull's hatred in the stare he gave me. I twisted down and out of that hold, pivoted, and would have swung, I think, if I hadn't looked directly at Wolves in Camp, who took a hold of my arm and didn't say a word.

I'd never spoken to the man. When he'd come silently to our camp along with Anna no more than a week before, he'd said maybe a dozen words. But I remembered his face because he was a man who looked—how can I

124

describe it?—maybe *solid* is the word, his oaklike face more square than round, his eyes clear and dark. He was young—probably twenty at most—but something strong and silent in his character made me believe he understood what I was thinking, and probably more. Short Bull commanded attention because he spoke with fire and passion; Wolves in Camp didn't need to say a word.

"We've been looking for you," I said. "We went toward Pine Ridge, then turned back. It's very dangerous out there, for us at least."

He made no gesture to indicate that he didn't understand.

"Dalitha is concerned about Anna," I told him. I had no idea what he did or didn't know. "They have been friends for many winters."

"You may speak to her," he said.

He wanted me to talk to her—that's what I remember.

He turned me slightly west, then walked with me through the throngs of people until I spotted her packing a travois. I don't know if he wanted the others to see him usher me there or if he wanted his hand on my arm to demonstrate that he had me under control—I don't know why he held on to me in that short walk we took, but he did. And then, twenty yards away, he let me go.

"You're not coming?" I said. When I called out, people looked around, so I walked back to him, because what I had to ask I didn't want spoken in a crowd. "Wolves in Camp," I said. "You are her husband?"

"I am her friend," he told me and then walked away.

125

I didn't have time to think about that right then because it was obvious Anna Crow did not intend to stay much longer at the Rosebud agency. She was lashing things down, whispering to the horse, keeping him still as she made the last adjustments. Flour, sugar, coffee, soap—it was all there. She looked no different from the last time I'd seen her; the loose-fitting, colorful shirt she wore gave no clear indication that she was carrying a child. But to see her tying down the goods on the travois, doing ordinary things, was a reminder of what it was about Anna Crow that had so scared Dalitha—a smile of overflowing peace that came from having given heart and soul, every bit of who she was, to the joy of following the messiah.

It seemed almost a sin to violate that peace, but I had so little time, certainly no time for pleasantries. "Wolves in Camp," I said, and she turned and looked at me as if snapped from a trance. "Is he the one who killed Dries Balkema?"

Her eyes narrowed and her smile fell away into something deeply sober as she dropped the leather straps and looked directly at me. Her whole face filled with something other than heavenly radiance.

"I know he is your friend," I said, "but if he—"

"He is my husband," she said.

"Your husband?"

She nodded, and the smile once more began to lift her face.

"He is the father of your child?" I asked.

She averted her eyes and reached for the straps on the travois.

It hurts me to say it now, but right then I would not let her retreat back into her faith. "Tell me, Anna Crow," I said, "this little one you will have—do you think it will be born before the messiah comes?"

She refused to look at me.

There were Sioux all around us. I had to stifle the anger that rose in me at her refusal to speak. I took a few steps closer and patted the horse's rump, as if I were friendly. "Is that what you hope for, Anna—that before the child comes, the buffalo will return and all of us will be gone?"

"You will all be gone," she told me. The warmth had vanished. "The dust will rise from our dancing, and you will be eaten up. The messiah has spoken it."

"His dream is not true, Anna," I told her. "When you feel in your body the pain only a woman knows, then you will know that this Paiute Wovoka is no more the Lord of heaven and earth than is this horse."

Something in her stiffened. "You put Jesus on a cross of shame," she said. "I know the story. For three winters I was in that school many sleeps from here, and I heard it many times." And then she came straight at me, as if unafraid. "His own put him on a cross, and now he has come to us because he knows our suffering and has heard our prayers. You turned your back on him."

Her blind faith only angered me more. "Why did Wolves in Camp have to kill Dries Balkema?" I said again. "To put silence over what it was you did with him?"

127

She stood tall and angry, and looked all around as if to make sure I remembered that she could, at any moment, call down the wrath of a dozen warriors.

"They're after him, you know," I said. "I have been there, in Friesland, and the people there know that some Sioux buck came across the river just to kill Dries. They know it, Anna. And who do you think they will suspect when suddenly you have a husband? They're coming after him already."

"Soon enough, the messiah will return," she told me confidently.

"And when he does, there will be no more weeping?" I said. "No more sadness. Is that right?" I was brutal to her, when I think of it now, very brutal, but I had so little time. "You tell me, Anna," I said, "this child you carry, will he be buried with us or will he reign with you? He is half *washechu*."

I saw not one hint of anything but resolve on her face. She didn't look at me, but neither did she look away.

"Or is it better simply to die?" I said.

"The messiah is coming."

"And what if he doesn't?"

"He will. The truth is in my heart. He will."

"Come with me," I said. "Come with us—with Sister Ward. There is danger here. There is so much danger."

"I am going with my people," she said. "We will dance until the messiah returns."

"And what if he doesn't, Anna?"

And then she smiled, the very smile that had slain Dalitha. "He told me that he will. He told me in a vision. I saw the face of the Great Mystery and his servant, the messiah."

I watched her tighten down whatever was still loose, then grab the reins of the sorrel pony beside the one pulling the travois and swing herself up on his back easily, as if she weren't pregnant at all. She pulled her blanket around her more tightly, looked back toward the stockade to find Wolves in Camp, and turned to me once more. "In my heart there is great joy," she said. "What is there in yours?"

And just like that, he was there—Wolves in Camp. I could have said so much more, but I think now that whatever I would have said would have been in vain. Anna Crow truly believed. Hers was a faith I could not break— nor could Dalitha.

I stood and watched them make their final preparations, and I wondered exactly why Wolves in Camp had gone out of his way to prompt me to talk to Anna Crow— as if it was something he had to do. What was his role— and why did each of them have a different answer about whether or not he was her husband?

As they mounted their horses and left the agency, somewhere in the hills a Hotchkiss roared. I'd seen them as we came in. Military maneuvers. They shot fistfuls of shrapnel, and that's why the Sioux used to say the Hotchkiss gun fired in the morning but killed the next day.

Whatever was passing through the minds of Anna Crow and Wolves in Camp as they left the Rosebud agency, whatever their relationship, whatever their plans for the future, what was clear to me at that moment, clearer than it had ever been before, was that their story—and ours, Dalitha and mine—was going to be but a small part of something bigger and much darker. That's what I heard in the Hotchkiss guns.

Maybe I felt it before—I don't remember exactly. I know that standing in the presence of the dancers scared me deeply. But not until that moment—not even when we were attacked by the Pine Ridge Oglalas—did I so clearly feel that the darkness all around would somehow cover us as well. In part, at least, it was Anna's radiant faith that made that darkness real.

I walked directly back to the agency office, where I suspected Dalitha was delivering some kind of sermon to whomever she could sit still to listen. I sat there on the steps and surveyed again the incredible activity going on all around me on a sloping plane that, just a decade ago, might have been the home for a single roving band of buffalo hunters and their families, a dozen tipis maybe, no more. The day was beautiful, like so many of them that early winter, but I could have cried, because it didn't take a prophet to see the clouds assembling in the open skies. Time alone would tell us what exactly would come from what was building everywhere we went.

God's hand brings storms—of that there is no doubt. But who would be the author of this destruction? Even if it came by way of the very hands I held before me—my own—could he not somehow stop it? Why wouldn't he? Those are questions that are never far from me, even these many years later.

"You won't believe it," Dalitha said when she came out of the agency's office. "You hear what they're doing, Jan? Shooting those guns? They're trying to put the fear of the Lord into these people, that's what they're doing. It's a show. It's a bare-knuckled show is what it is, and it's meant to make them cower!"

Dalitha had come out of the office. That I sat right there beneath her seemed not to surprise her at all, but then she was so angry she couldn't think straight. She was not really speaking to me anyway, but hoping what she was saying would get back into the agency office through the windows, even though it was November and nothing was open.

"You know what I heard in there? They're recruiting hundreds of Sioux police, hundreds of them, giving them good coats and food and a badge for a promise of loyalty. Divide and conquer. Feed those who promise loyalty. Make them agency police, make them peacemakers. When the army's involved, there's only an iron fist on the reservation." She attracted the attention of people milling around, which was something she was after. "You and I, Jan—we can't leave," she said. "'It's too dangerous for you out there,' the colonel said. 'Too dangerous?' I said. 'I have lived here for fifteen years, and you're telling me what I can and can't do?' That's what I told him, and you know what he said? He said, 'I'm ordering you not to leave the agency.'" Her eyes went everywhere. "We're prisoners here. You and I, we're being 'detained,' he said. What a wonderful word—*detained*. Sounds almost fancy, doesn't it?"

I had to get her attention, so I got to my feet and took hold of her arm. "Listen," I said. "Anna Crow and Wolves in Camp—they just now left, going north."

She reached for my wrist, then looked around quickly, as if Anna and Wolves in Camp were somewhere just down the street in front of the office.

"They're gone," I told her. "I watched them leave."

She threw off my hand. "You didn't stop them?"

I shook my head.

"You didn't even talk to them?"

"I spoke to both of them," I said.

"'Spoke to them'? What does that mean?"

"I tried to reason—"

"You can't reason with them," she said. "You heard her. Her reason is gone, Jan. She doesn't *think* anymore."

"I should have knocked her down? I should have knocked both of them down and lugged them back here to you?"

She raised both hands up over her eyes, stood for a moment in silence, then let them slide slowly down until her fingertips covered her lips. "I'm sorry," she whispered.

"You have reason to be angry."

132

"Not at you," she said, and she reached for my arm, held it just momentarily, then took a breath. "We must go after her, of course."

"We're being detained," I said.

"We have to go after her."

"For Christ's sake?" I said.

She knew exactly what I meant. She reached up and ran her fingers through her hair. "Yes," she said. "Of course, for Christ's sake. Is there someone else in charge here?"

"You," I said. "*Your* will. I don't think we should get the two confused."

When I think of what I may have become had I not met Dalitha Ward, I shudder—not because I was on the road to dissolution, but because I was already some distance toward real despair. That she brought me happiness goes without saying, but what she did in those first years especially was give me cause to live. She had so much cause herself that simply being in her presence was like adding a pair of lungs and another beating heart. I don't know that I really thought so at the time, but when I remember how angry she was at that moment, I think I can safely say that there were times she needed me as much as I needed her.

"We just let them go?" she said.

"She believes everything will be fine once the messiah comes," I told her. "She believes that every care will vanish when we disappear into the earth. And he's coming soon."

133

"We can't let her believe that," Dalitha said.

"Her will is not ours to own."

"So we simply let her go?"

"And pray."

She looked at me strangely. "Jan Ellerbroek," she said, "I don't know that I've ever heard you say that."

"I did what I could," I said. "I even lied to her. What else can we do?"

"What did you say?"

"I don't think it matters what I said," I told her. "She believes all things come together for good for those who love Wovoka."

"I don't care," she said. "I'm not staying. Arrest or detention or whatever, I'm not staying here, because all of them—" she pointed to the Sioux outside the gates, many still getting and packing their rations, "all of them will believe that the army is here to destroy them if I have to stay, because if Sister Ward and her husband are locked up in the agency, if we can't go home, they will believe for sure that the army is ready to kill them all—for Custer, for gold, for whatever reason. Maybe just for hate. And if they believe that, who knows what they will do?"

She was right. About that, she was absolutely right. "I'll get the wagon," I told her.

No one stopped us as we moved through the gates. There were too many people moving in and out of the agency that day for the army to take notice of everything. I don't know if they would have held their rifles up to us

to make us reconsider, and I don't know what Dalitha
would have done had they forced us to stay. But we left
without anyone trying to keep us there, and I set the
course east toward the Missouri.

"May I see her at least?" Dalitha said.

I didn't doubt we could catch them, so I turned north
and drove beside a long phalanx of Sioux men and women
and children lugging rations back to their camps. They
didn't use roads—there weren't any to speak of; they
merely fanned out into the crackling grasses north of the
agency.

I told Dalitha we would look, but once we were a half
mile away, I doubted that we'd see the two of them—
there was just too much space.

But we did. We came to the top of a knoll and looked
down, and there they were, riding, each of them on a
pony, a third beside them pulling the travois. Wolves in
Camp had to have been, by Sioux standards, a young man
of some means. I tugged on the reins, and the wagon
creaked to a stop. Only if they had looked around and
really searched would they have seen us.

"So now what will happen?" Dalitha said.

When I think of it now—that picture of the two of them
riding off north—what I still see is Anna Crow's shoulders and perfectly squared back. She rode with grace and
dignity and almost effortless conviction. She had so much
of what I'd lost, deeply rooted in a wondrous dream of
hope that was only that—a wondrous dream. She had
the faith that I lacked.

"I don't know what will happen," I told Dalitha. "But I know this much—something in her has to break. It's just as you said—something is going to have to break inside her. But neither of us will do it, not you or me. It will have to be something bigger."

"She's carrying a child," Dalitha said.

Reason, even when laced with falsehood like my story about the Friesland people creating a lynch mob, had no effect on Anna Crow. It deflected off her insistent faith like so many meaningless words. I was ready to leave and return home, because I was convinced there was nothing we could do now but wait—and pray. And that's what I did, right there on the hill as the two of them moved out slowly into the grayness of a winter that was already too long in coming. I spoke to a God who hadn't listened to my own fervent prayers in the past. I came to him again with another request for life.

"She's going to have a baby, Jan," Dalitha said again, as if I hadn't heard.

"Maybe that's our only hope," I told her.

# ❧ Seven ❧

When the weather finally turned cold, I thought our problems would be over. So did Dalitha. Dakota winters are no time to dance. It had been—and I know I've said this before—a remarkably warm fall and early winter; however, that was not terribly unusual either, for when the winter winds slide down off the Rockies in the far west, often as not those winds keep us warmer than the farmers east of the Missouri and in Iowa. But suddenly in December, the temperature dropped to near zero, and I remember thinking that the newly arrived winter cold was an answer to prayer.

When we returned home, there was another letter from my father, announcing his arrival across the river on the 11th. "We," he wrote, and I assumed he meant himself and my mother, which somewhat surprised me, because it was difficult to imagine her—an upper-class Dutch lady, after all—coming out to the edge of the frontier. He mentioned nothing else, really, except to say that they wanted to see me and my new wife.

The only clue I had about what was to happen was suggested by the single word *need*: "We *need* to see you," he wrote, which I found puzzling. And he'd written in English for some reason, not in Dutch, probably for Dalitha's sake, and I simply assumed he meant it the way it sounded. "We will look for you then," my father wrote. "We *need* to see you."

I knew it could not be a pleasure trip; not in his life did my father ever embark on something so frivolous as a vacation. At that time, he was still hard at work trying to establish a new church and new denomination, attending to his flock in a little church in Noordeloos, Michigan, somewhere along the lakeshore, somewhere not far from where my first wife and our little girls were buried.

Something in me wanted to go back to Friesland on my own. I didn't know for sure that Dalitha did not want to go along, but I knew that at this time, going another whole day east, away from the reservation, would be difficult for her.

On the reservations just west of the river, things had quieted some, although a few Sioux parents told Dalitha that their children would not be coming to school because they had gone to church. They meant the dancing, and the reason they gave was not a lie. They were telling the truth as they saw it, because the messiah in whom they'd come to believe was as real to them as Jesus was to those most fervently praying for his coming across the river in Friesland, and farther east in Douglas County, in Harrison and New Holland.

With school to attend to and children to teach but with Anna Crow unaccounted for somewhere and pregnant with the child of a father already buried for more than a month, Dalitha remained very anxious and suffered from cabin fever. Always there were rumors of unrest, even though the reservation was full of bluecoats. Maybe the unrest was because of them.

Late at night Dalitha tried to take up some mending, weaving, other household tasks, but she was never destined to take joy from such mundane things. In a way, I have to laugh at it now when I remember her making sweetbread and "fluffing the nest," as they say; it was all meant to fill the hours and quell her anxiousness. She tried to be the dutiful wife in order to relieve her fears, but her mind and soul and heart were west of our cabin, with the people she'd come to serve and grown to love, and especially with a wandering young woman she believed was her own personal responsibility.

I heard her swear one night. I don't think I'd ever heard her do that before. She was making tea when she dropped a cup. We had no precious things—it was simply a cup, but it was full, and just like that, the kitchen floor was awash with hot tea. And she used, aloud, a common earthy expression.

I laughed. Not out loud, though. I knew better.

Our cabin was unpretentious, in part, I suppose, because it's difficult to be pretentious on the prairie. Two rooms, really, that's all—a bedroom and what remained. What I'm saying is that it was impossible for me not to have heard. I was reading something, I imagine, and the shock of it—not the broken cup, but her vulgarity—made me laugh.

Then there was more. No attempt to hide either. She aimed that word at me, repeated it ten times like the fire from a machine gun to make sure there was no mistaking my hearing it.

"Let me clean it up," I said.

"Don't you dare, Jan Ellerbroek. Don't you dare."

So I watched. She threw nothing, said nothing. She pulled the bucket from beside the stove, poured in some water, armed herself with a rag, drew up the hem of her skirt, got on her knees, and wiped up the tea, never looking up, never saying anything. Her hands moved methodically, as if all her anger and frustration had left her in that torrent of barnyard language.

When she was finished, she pulled herself back to her feet, grabbed the pail, walked to the door, stepped outside, and threw out the contents. Then she stepped back in. Not once did she look at me; I could have been a bookshelf, a candle, a fly on the wall. I would have liked to have been a fly on the wall.

Then she drew a chair back from the table and sat in silence, stony-faced, almost emotionless, but ready, I knew, to erupt once again. I looked back down at my book because it was clear she was not going to address me with her eyes. I pretended to read. Five minutes passed, maybe more, maybe less.

140

"We have to go after her, Jan," she said finally.

I looked up. She was staring toward the door. I can remember that with Rinska it was the same—in marriage, sometimes things have to be said even if they're not meant. Dalitha needed to say that to me, even if she knew better herself. We'd been through it before—how it was silly and dangerous to go after Anna Crow. We had no idea where she was. Anna was a woman, not a girl, and she'd determined by faith to follow Wovoka, to put her training school behind her, to take Wolves in Camp, to dance until the messiah returned. Aside from kidnapping her, we could do nothing. I went over all of that in my mind again but said nothing.

"You think I'm crazy," she said, not asking a question.

That's when I got up from the chair, walked over to the table, and sat down beside her. "You're right," I told her. "I think you're crazy."

She looked at me. "If it wasn't for you, I'd be on the horse right now," she said. "I wouldn't be here anymore." Then she pointed west.

"Then go," I told her. "I don't want to be a burden."

Her icy stare softened. She looked down and folded her hands in front of her, and I took them in mine. And there we sat in silence until it became clear to me that nothing I could say would be anything she wouldn't have thought of herself. Nothing.

Except this. I swore—just once. And I don't know if the word she had said and the one I echoed was really *swearing*—it's a barnyard word my father would have disapproved of, but it's a word spoken frequently on the farms around Friesland. I just said it, and then, when a smile finally broke on her face, I repeated it, maybe ten times, just as she had.

And then we laughed—both of us.

And then we prayed—both of us.

And I'm telling you this little story because the story you wanted me to tell is, as I've said, very much my own story too. I can't separate mine from yours. This was a moment when I really did want to pray; so often in the years after Rinska's death—and the death of my own beautiful daughters—I didn't want to address our Father in heaven, hallowed be his name.

But that night in our cabin, the two of us sat together, our hands folded in each other's over the table. And I prayed. I wanted to pray, perhaps because I had reached the point where there was nothing I could say anymore but the barnyard word.

I don't remember the prayer, nor hers. But what I'll not forget is that it was very real and that I meant it, probably because out there on a reservation that was coming apart, that suffered from fear and danger and deprivation and poverty, there was nothing left to say and nothing left to do but wait upon the Lord.

I'd done some odd jobs for a while on the west side of the Missouri, then contracted with the agency to get some supplies that had come in from the railhead at Plankington. I didn't want to be gone from Dalitha for long periods of time—maybe that was silly of me. I don't doubt that I needed her more than she needed me.

One day, on a quick trip across the river, I ran into Felician Fallas. Outfitted in leather the way I was, I'm sure I didn't look like a Hollander, most of whom were sodbusters. I know I didn't talk like one either, having been born in America some years after my parents left the Netherlands. That day, I was coming east across the river from the reservation, and it never would have occurred to him that I was a Dutchman, since all of the Hollanders he knew were homesteading east of the Missouri, many of them more than a day's ride away, few of them interested in whatever it was that lay beyond the river to the west. I was a lone man with a wagon, obviously a drayman. He simply wouldn't have guessed that I could be one of what he called "the wooden heads." And I didn't tell him. I let him talk.

The two of us were aboard Nick Fordham's ferry, an old horse-powered flatboat that made regular runs between Charles Mix on the east and Gregory County on the west side of the river.

The Missouri River isn't that much different from the reservation, when I come to think about it. Most of the time it's smooth and quiet. Fordham's team of horses was stepping off paces on that treadmill almost as regular as clockwork, now and then a whinny or two, a roll of water from the prow barely making a sound. Peaceful as the prairie.

Oddly enough, as you know, few places in this land can offer the comforting silence of the reservation. That December, in those few weeks when Dalitha and I were waiting for news of Anna Crow, out in the open spaces I sometimes told myself that with nothing more than the company of meadowlarks and coyotes in the unending openness, I too could be a brother to God's creatures, like the Sioux. Coming to the Rosebud when I did, I had missed the buffalo, the numberless herds that roamed the grasslands as free as those who'd hunted them and even worshipped them. Countless times I came upon the old bleached skulls that seemed almost to blossom from the short grass. With all those skulls and all that peace, even though I never saw a herd, I believe I could have been counted among those *washechu* who, in our own dim way, understood how bison could be worshipped.

Often, the river, like the reservation, seemed reverent with peace, and it was on that day—until I met Fallas, who must have taken one look at me and decided that, unlike the Hollanders, I was savvy enough to know the truth.

"You too will be affected," Fallas told me, a prominent finger poking in my face. He was a Frenchman, a survivor of the old fur-trading days, an Indian War veteran who'd worked as a scout for the military as far back as Little Big Horn. Tall and lanky, dressed far better than most of those who lived near the river, he sat one leg over the other, looking out at the line of hills on the west side of the river.

144

"When Fort Randall closes, it will be the end of it—for you *and* me," he said. Then he spread his hands wide. "And all of this, all of these good people here who come now to America, the dream will be only a mirage, because it will be over." He drew a finger across his throat.

Fallas owned considerable timber along the river, at least the land we were looking at right then, and he did a brisk business with Fort Randall to the south. If the fort were to close, as the government had said, then it would be the end of his own big contracts.

"And it's not a lie either," he told me, pointing west. "You know, the reservation is boiling over."

He didn't wait for me to comment because he wasn't looking for my opinion.

He turned to look east, toward the white settlements. "Every one of them, you know, they all live in fear of the redskins." Then a belly laugh. He spun his hand in the air like a magician. "I tell them—those dumb Swedes and Bohunks and the wooden head Hollanders—I tell them that unless they sign the petition to keep the fort open, the redskins will go wild, because they will." He looked at me as if he was working on a stump speech. "And in all of their hearts, you know, there is deep, deep fear." And then another laugh. "And, of course, they sign the petition."

"Maybe it's not a lie—what you tell them," I said to Fallas. "Maybe someday soon the hostiles will ride across the river right here and burn everything."

"You know better," he told me. "Already there are too many of us here." He gave me a knowing wink. "The government is a fat cow," he said. Once more, he raised his finger. "There is, you know, far more milk in fat cows."

"So you do well among the Hollanders?" I said. "They line up to sign your petition, I suppose?"

He nodded, grudgingly. "But they don't trust me."

I acted surprised. "Is that true? Why not?"

"I'm a papist," he said, his eyes bulging as if the revelation was astounding.

"Fallas," I said, "you are no more a Catholic than I am a Sioux. How many wives have you by now?" It was rumored he had at least four.

Two hands came up quickly to his chest as if the question were an affront. "You cannot believe what you hear. And what again was your name?"

I told him Jan—that's all.

"If someone believes everything he hears on the river, Jan," he said, "then that man is a fool."

"Like the Hollanders," I said.

A huge laugh exploded from him. "Yes, yes," he said. "You must have heard that as we speak, Mr. William Cody is going after old Sitting Bull? Sent by the president himself—Buffalo Bill will bring the old buck to surrender, and that will be it with this messiah madness."

"And that will be it for Fort Randall," I told him.

He moved closer to me, put his arm around my shoulders, then pointed at my wagon. "You and me, we can't let that happen," he said. "Think of what it would mean

146

here—no more business for you either. Think of it—it would spell the end of so many things." Almost as if he carried a stiletto, he once again made a swipe across his throat. Then his eyes lit up. "So maybe you would like to come with me now into the wooden-head villages and speak to them, get them to sign." He patted the leather bag hanging from his shoulder. "It is, after all, for their own good."

"They know me," I told him.

"Then all the better," he said, slapping my back. "They trust you, I'm sure."

"Fallas," I said, "I worship with them."

"Noooo," he said. He honestly wouldn't believe me. "Where are your wooden shoes?" he said, pointing at my boots.

I tapped my forehead. "I used them for my wooden head." I smiled, and he laughed because he still didn't believe what I'd said. I knew I had to prove it. What came to me was the psalm from Balkema's funeral, something from Psalm 116, a line that had become fixed in my memory. I recited the lines in Dutch.

> *God heb ik lief: want die getrouwe HEER*
> *Hoort mijne stem, miijn smeekingen, mijn klagen;*
> *Hij schenkt mij hulp, Hij redt mij keer op keer.*

Those huge eyes of his nearly rolled out of their sockets.

More came to me. I spoke hurriedly, but not without some anger.

147

*Ik lag gekneld in banden van den dood,*
*Daar d'angst der hell' mij allen troost deed missen;*
*Ik was benaauwd, omringd door droefenissen;*
*Maar riep den HEER dus aan in al mijn' nood.*

For a moment, he sat in stunned silence. But Felician Fallas had stood up to Crazy Horse and Sitting Bull and who knows how many gamblers, thieves, and cutthroats more crooked than himself. He nodded. "Well, it is for *their* good, you know," he told me, that finger pointed again. "I don't care who your people are; if Fort Randall goes, all of this goes too." Once more he swept his arm over the kingdom east of the river, the kingdom he wanted to rule. "It is true," he said, and then he walked away, muttering.

That line of the psalm, it had come to me in the same way that we put our hands or arms out when we stumble, as if by instinct. I'm sure that Fallas understood not a word of it, of course, but it was clear to him that I wasn't who he thought I was. But then I'm not so very sure I knew right then which one of us was the greatest deceiver.

From Fallas I'd heard something of the story of Sitting Bull, a story that would play a much larger role in all of this I'm telling you. Even though the old holy man was the most famous Indian on the reservations at the time, I don't remember a single Sioux man or woman my wife really disliked except him. His fame may well have been part of the reason for her dislike—I hesitate to call what she felt *hate* because I'm not sure she ever knew him well enough to hate him. She had simply seen him here and there, and had heard of him because everyone knew of Sitting Bull. A few years earlier he had spent some time not far from our cabin, in the jail at Fort Randall. He and his band, nearly destitute, had surrendered to the military after a few years' exile in Canada, where they'd escaped following the battle at Little Big Horn. He was something of a chief, something of a holy man, and, for a time at least, perhaps the most famous of Buffalo Bill's showboat Indians in those Wild West touring shows.

The reason Dalitha disliked him, I think, is that she saw him more as a politician than a leader of his people. Her faith back then—and even today—was in ordinary people, what the Dutch used to call the *kleine volk,* the little people. Maybe it was his tours with Buffalo Bill in New York—signing autographs for a dollar—that made her distrust him. To her, Sitting Bull was not *kleine volk*.

But I was anxious to tell Dalitha what I'd heard from Fallas the fearmonger, who'd told me that Buffalo Bill was bringing Sitting Bull into the army as one of the last—and certainly the most famous—of the hostiles.

I'd picked up some wood from the river flats on the way home, because no Dakotan ever believes fully in Mother Nature's pleasantries, no matter how sweet the charm of autumn's lingering warmth. Dalitha had not yet returned from school that afternoon, so I unloaded my cargo on the woodpile beneath the lean-to I'd set up in back of the cabin, and was still at it when she returned.

It gives me some pleasure to remember those days now, even though we feared what was happening all around us. Dalitha walked out back, stood with her hands on her hips, and watched me unload for a moment, then smiled. "You know," she said, "I've become accustomed to having men stack firewood for me. I don't believe I've ever done it myself."

It was cottonwood, light wood, burned like paper.

"You had men here for all those years?" I said. "How is it a man never learns these things until *after* the wedding?"

She walked up to me and kissed me. "If it's any consolation," she said, "you're the first one I've ever kissed." She grabbed both of my shoulders and straightened my jacket as if sending me off to church. "So what's the news among the Dutch?" she said.

"I'm still the lost sheep," I told her, "and you're still Delilah."

She stepped back, arched her shoulders, and pursed her lips. "Delilah?" she said, loosening the ties on her hat and slipping it from her head.

"'Delilah,' they tell me, and then they stare out over my shoulder as if gazing into the very face of evil."

"You're the one who's ruined *me,* you know," she said. "With you around here, what I was is not what I am."

"Here, maybe," I told her, still throwing logs on the pile, "but in Friesland and Castalia, you're the one who ruined me."

"Then we're both sinners."

"Ah, you've become a Calvinist."

"Jan Ellerbroek," she said, "don't say that. I haven't fallen that far." She tied the string of her bonnet to the wagon wheel, hoisted herself up on the back of the wagon, and began handing me the firewood.

We were working together, the sun setting as early as it always does in December, when I told her what Fallas, whom she knew far better than I did, had told me about Buffalo Bill himself having been enlisted to bring Sitting Bull into McLaughlin, the agent at Standing Rock.

"What is this, vaudeville?" she said.

I grew up speaking English, but I had no idea what she meant. "Vaudeville?" I said.

"I forget you grew up in the New Jerusalem," she told me. "It means . . . what?—how can I explain it?—cheap entertainment, entertainment of the worst kind, entertainment that the Calvinists warned you about, I'm sure, day and night."

"You don't think bringing in Sitting Bull is a good idea?"

She stopped for a moment and lifted her hand to smooth back her hair. "Maybe it is," she said. "If anyone else tries to bring in that old trickster, it might just anger his band." She nodded. "It makes sense, even though it sounds more like a Wild West show."

What we knew was that Sitting Bull's band, way up at Standing Rock, several days' travel from where we lived on the Rosebud, was one of the last bands of traditionalists, those who adamantly refused to scratch the earth or be beholden to the reservation system of annuities. Short Bull and Kicking Bear had brought them the Ghost Dance. Nowhere else was the messiah craze as wild as it

151

was at Sitting Bull's camp at Standing Rock. That's what people said.

"It's a risk," she said, taking up more wood. "His people may see Sitting Bull's leaving his camp as a much greater threat, no matter who it is that brings him in—Cody and his show horse or some cavalry bluecoats."

"And what do you think?" I said.

Once more, she stopped. She shrugged her shoulders, rubbed dirt from her hands. "I think we still need to pray for snow. Nothing will end this madness so quickly as real winter."

Later, in the cabin, we once again talked about what might be happening. "I don't trust him," she said.

"Cody?"

"Sitting Bull. He's an old holy man. It's hard for me to believe that he would have any great faith in the whole Wovoka vision, because it's so, well, *washechu* in its own way."

She was right. We didn't know it then, but what Dalitha had presumed was the truth. Sitting Bull was far less a believer in the Ghost Dance than were the hundreds, if not thousands, of Sioux who had visions in the late fall of 1890, but he was smart enough to understand the benefits the messiah craze could offer him.

"You're coming along to meet my folks?" I asked her a little later.

"Promise to make them speak English," she said. "You know how much I dislike it when you speak to each other in Dutch."

152

"I'm not sure they can speak English that well," I told her.

"Well, then, teach them."

From what cubbyhole in my memory the phrase came from, I suppose I'll never know; but there it was, almost instantly. *"Oude beren dansen leren is zwepen verknoeien,"* I told her.

She looked at me and hunched her shoulders.

"It means something like 'old dogs and new tricks,'" I said. And then I thought through it, the old words, the old language. "Something like this—'If you try to teach old bears to dance, you'll only ruin good whips.'"

The ancient Dutch proverb fit Sitting Bull as well—the old man who must have looked on the fierce dancing and blind faith as irrelevant to him but something he could use to his advantage. Many of his people thought of him as a hero of Little Big Horn, even though he'd never taken up a bow or a lance. He stayed in the background, a spiritual leader who'd predicted Custer's great loss. He stayed in the background of the messiah craze as well, until he couldn't anymore. But when he became a part of the movement, his story and eventual martyrdom inflamed the fires already burning in the hearts of those who truly believed.

On the Rosebud, the fanaticism had been doused by the menacing presence of hundreds of bluecoats. But with Christmas approaching, with winter as reluctant to make an appearance as I ever remember, with the pregnant Anna Crow and her friend/husband Wolves in

Camp somewhere far away, and with none other than the world's most famous cowboy enlisted to bring in Sitting Bull, we didn't know what would happen. No one did.

Only God knew what would happen, which is something I find difficult to admit, even today.

That night at supper, Dalitha asked the Lord, as always, for the coming of winter. But that did not mean the Lord turned his face upon us and gave us peace by way of snow. A very short period of winter cold, early December, was followed by more warmth, the winds blowing gently from the west and carrying unseasonable temperatures. In any other year we would have thought it a measure of his grace.

There was a lull during that time, enough so that Dalitha had little to do and therefore assumed a visit to the Dutch colonies east of the river was preferable to the isolation she'd feel without me. What's more, she knew my parents would believe it only right and proper that a good wife accompany her husband to Harrison, Douglas County, where they would be staying.

She didn't hide her discomfort at our crossing the Missouri and heading east, but neither did she needle or *zannik,* since she didn't need to tell me how moving east away from the reservation did not give her joy. It wasn't simply my people that made her bad-tempered, it was the westward movement of the homesteaders— all of them—that seemed a poison to her soul. For her, encroaching settlements forecasted the end of everything she'd worked for and only greater misery among the people she loved.

We left on a Friday. I wanted to get to Friesland that day, then continue farther east and reach Harrison by Saturday night. A second letter from my father indicated they would be in Harrison, which back then was the heart of the Dutch community. We would spend the Sabbath with my parents—and worship with them, of course—stay over Monday, then start back on Tuesday. That was our plan.

It was Friday afternoon when we came to Fordham's crossing, and it was Nick himself, not his son-in-law who normally ran the ferry, who ushered us across. His trusted team stepped off their paces and powered us across the quiet waters of a river we well might have forded ourselves, so low was the water that winter.

Dalitha hadn't said much since we'd left our place, so I was surprised when, once aboard, she brought up the name of Dries Balkema. She mentioned him because it occurred to her that if Dries had seen Anna Crow often enough to fall in love, he'd have crossed over to the west side of the river often; and if he had, he would have likely used Nick Fordham's ferry. "You know a man—a young man, a Hollander—named Balkema?" she asked Nick Fordham.

Fordham didn't need to steer the ferry all that much. That day the Missouri seemed no more dangerous than an old milk cow.

"Too bad what happened," he said, not really looking at us at all.

155

"He was too young to die," I said.

"He's dead?" Fordham said, obviously shocked.

"I thought you knew," I told him. "A month or so already."

He shook his head. "Hollanders hung him, I suppose?" Then he looked at me because he knew where I'd come from. "Sorry. But sometimes I'd choose to be blown away by a cyclone rather than have to deal with their self-righteousness."

"Why would they have hung him?" I said.

Then he told us the story that helped us put together how it was that a boy from the Dutch colony had been able to get close to a reservation girl, close enough to make a baby, an act well outside the moral codes of both their people.

"She was a short hair," he told us.

Anna Crow had been to boarding school out East. Anna Crow had short hair.

"Only once did I catch a glimpse of her when he came back across the river." He pulled the pipe he was smoking from his mouth and blew lightly on the ashes.

"They were together?" Dalitha said.

"It was a joy to bring him back," Fordham said. "Sometimes I did it for free. For an old man like me," he said with a smile, "sometimes just to be in the presence of young love, it's a very good thing." He nodded. "And he was in love, this Balkema boy—or so it seemed, at least until the end."

There must have been an end—that's what I thought.

156

"He's dead, you say?" Fordham asked, looking at me.

I think he asked because he didn't want to break some confidence. When I nodded, he went on.

"The last time it was like the other times, on the Sabbath—not many Hollanders ride the ferry on the Sabbath, you know. But the last time, the music in him had stopped. His eyes were dark as night, full of clouds, and he said nothing." He turned his foot and hit that pipe against his heel, the dying ashes spilling over the planks beneath us. "So I was the one who spoke. He was just a boy, you know, and I looked forward to him coming back, because he could . . ." Then he stopped and looked at both of us as if to gauge whether or not he could trust us. "It was love that lit up the night," he said. He shook his head. "I sound like a woman."

"Tell us," Dalitha said.

"Like I said, it was me who spoke, and I pointed up there," he said and pointed for us up on the bank of the east side, adjacent to his place. "See that gate, that fence?" he said. "That's where my wife is buried. I buried her myself twelve years ago with these hands."

Fordham was one of the few pioneers on the river. He'd been there long before there were any white colonies.

"So I said to him—this is what I said—I said, 'It's now a dozen years since I buried my wife up there on the hill. You can see her grave.' And I told him that not one hour of the day passed without I feel a dark shadow cross my soul."

I didn't know what he was getting at.

157

"And the boy looked up at me, and his face was all sadness, his eyes ringed and cloudy and red." He drew imaginary lines around his eyes. "Maybe he was embarrassed. I don't know. But I thought to myself that it had ended, whatever it was that he'd come across the river so often to get." He pulled himself to his feet and spoke to the horses, then turned back to us. "And I said to him, I said, 'Boy, my wife who is buried up there on the hill, she was Sioux. I'm a squaw man, and I'm proud—and I loved her.' And that was the last time I saw him."

What was clear was that the story about Dries Balkema knowing a young woman from the reservation was true. What Arie Boon claimed Balkema had confessed before dying was likely also true. And Dalitha had probably been right in assuming the girl was Anna Crow. Of course, we had presumed all of that to be true for so long that what Fordham told us didn't change our minds about anything. But it did make it clear that Dries had not forced himself on the girl, as Dalitha once had thought. What's more, the old man's description of the boy's face upon his return had me believing that what Dries had looked for across the Missouri wasn't something he alone had sought. Anna Crow had as well.

"How could they have met?" Dalitha said.

"He told me once," Fordham said. "He said she had come with some of her people from the Yankton reservation—after *wakpamni*," he said.

*Wakpamni* was the winter distribution of clothes and blankets and annuities. Often whole families would come east to sell those things to the homesteaders, who were often no less needy than their Indian neighbors.

Anna Crow, just back from boarding school, with her short hair, must have made it clear to Dries that she was not one of the tribe anymore. She would have looked different, she would have spoken differently, because, as she had already told us, she knew she was different.

"And when was it, this last time when he came back so sad?" Dalitha asked.

"It was summer. The cottonwood leaves were noisy, I remember, like they can be in the summer wind." He pointed up at the empty branches of the trees along the river. "Early summer maybe, some time ago already."

"And you didn't see him again?" I said.

He shook his head, then chuckled. "I'm an old man," he said. "I have seen things on this river that you wouldn't believe and wouldn't want to remember." He came back and sat beside us once again. "But that boy— it was a great joy to bring him back and forth across the Mud."

"He could have forded," Dalitha said.

"This last summer, without rain—I don't have to tell you—lots of people don't need my ferry. But this boy, I think he wanted to come with me because he trusted me. And besides, he had money." He raised both hands up as if surprised. "You know as well as I do that the Hollanders don't pay their help so well, but this boy had money."

Arie Boon wouldn't have been a big spender. I knew that. But I had no idea where Dries Balkema would have gotten his money.

"I think he wanted to come across the river with me," he told Dalitha. "Maybe I just wish that was true. It is sad to think he's gone."

# ❧ Eight ❧

Nick Fordham's remark about how the Hollanders might have killed Dries Balkema for his love of a girl from the wrong side of the river was something Dalitha quickly latched on to. Once we left the ferry, she made that very clear.

"It's amazing to me that I never thought of it," she told me.

"A lynching? You think it was a lynching?" I said. "Maybe right in the horse barn of the church—a whole bunch of Dutchmen carrying torches maybe, their women taunting him before he died, prayer and coffee served up afterward."

"You know, Jan, it doesn't take a rope to do a lynching," she said angrily.

"Don't forget Wolves in Camp," I told her.

"You honestly believe that young man rode all the way over here and shot this Balkema out of . . . what? Out of jealousy? That's nonsense."

161

"It's nonsense as well to think that Friesland people killed him in some fit of righteous anger," I told her.

For a long time we didn't speak.

The hours of daylight had shrunk as if to nothing by mid-December. I am reminded now of some of the strange ideas the Sioux have about dusk, how it is full of illusions, things not there at all. By the time we'd covered the miles that separated the river from the Friesland church, it was already dusk. And it was cold—or perhaps what I am remembering is the air surrounding the wagon. There, at least, the temperature was zero.

The first homestead east of the river belonged to a man named Siepke Eerkes, who, like several of the other immigrant families from the early settlement, was by birth unflinchingly upper class, despite the fact that he lived on next to nothing on the Dakota grasslands. I remember how his daughters, in those first years, sometimes tended the hogs in their old country finery. If I hadn't noticed what I did when we approached his place, I wouldn't have stopped, because Siepke was the kind of man who—by reason of his convictions—fulfilled all of Dalitha's worst suspicions about Dutch people.

There were no lamps lit, no signs of life anywhere except the livestock milling about. Someone passing west to east would certainly have drawn the attention of the family, especially the children. But no one emerged from the tiny frame house or the lean-to out back. Linens and bedding were spread over the grass and left to whiten in the sun; but the sun was long gone. It was unlike the

162

Eerkes family—or any of the immigrants for that matter—
to leave work undone.

I turned down the lane, fully expecting to see someone
emerge from the door of the cabin, but all around the
yard there was nothing but silence, save the clutter of
noise from the unprotected chicken house. Two cows
seemed ready for milking, but it appeared as if they'd not
been looked after.

"Maybe they're at church," Dalitha said.

I told her not in the afternoon—and on a Friday.

"A funeral," she said.

It was possible, but the yard looked far too abandoned.

And so it was with the next two places we passed, both
of them left empty, as if in the middle of a working day
the family had simply decided to pick up and leave the
prairie. When we finally came up over a rise and spotted
the church, I realized Dalitha had been right: They were
all at church. Weddings didn't take place in church back
then, so I assumed that Dalitha was right about the
funeral too.

We were still a distance from the church, where lamps
were lit, when a man in a Dutch cap poked his shotgun
at us. I had no idea who this man was; even back then
people moved in and out of those communities as if the
land were a horse no one could break. The gun in our
faces was frightening, but the man's language, as I remember, left the two of us laughing.

"Up the hands," he said gruffly.

Dalitha giggled—I swear it.

"What here you like to do?" he said.

"Are you crazy?" I said, but in the Dutch. *"Ben je gek?"*
Immediately he lowered the gun.

They were holed up in church, the whole neighbor-hood, waiting for swarming red devils to swoop down from the hills along the Mud in search of scalps. Inside, there were only a few guns but lots of pitchforks and an assortment of hatchets and Bowie knives. And, of course, there was fear.

Their fright was partly related to Sitting Bull's capture, partly to the general uneasiness caused by the messiah craze, partly to men like Fallas who spread fear for their own ends. But you know too that it's easy to be fright-ened out here, in a world where it seems there is no place to hide. Indian scares happened more often back then—and it was happening in Friesland the moment we'd arrived.

Abraham Brinks, seeing us, simply assumed we'd pulled up stakes out west as a result of painted hostiles. "Jan," he said, giving me a bear hug, as unusual among the Dutch as it is among the Sioux, "what news?"

"Go home," I told him in the Holland language. "Your cows need milking."

Thirty people, maybe forty, half of them children or young people, stared at the two of us who'd just arrived up from the west, from the land of the hostiles. I think there was more shock than relief on their faces when we told them there was nothing to be afraid of. Some of them—people who didn't know me—were deeply skeptical; after all, I didn't look like them, even if I could speak their language. And the woman beside me, sharp-eyed and dressed like an American, didn't look Dutch.

Brinks, who was deeply devout, was nonetheless capable of listening to reason. "Ever since Dries Balkema," he told us, "we've been afraid, you know." He spoke English so Dalitha could understand. "And we hear things always." He shrugged his shoulders, as if embarrassed. "Did you know that Cody failed—that he didn't bring in Sitting Bull?"

We'd heard the story, but the tale of what had actually happened arrived in the Friesland neighborhood with a different twist. McLaughlin, the agent at Standing Rock, had worked tirelessly to get Buffalo Bill off the reservation before he could create any damage, and he'd succeeded. What Brinks had heard—and what they all had innocently believed—was what Buffalo Bill had said when he left Bismarck on the train: his being removed from the job meant there would be hell to pay.

"Who told you? Fallas?" I said.

Brinks nodded.

"And this?" I pointed at the people huddled behind him. Their fear couldn't have all been a result of Sitting Bull.

"Rumors," he said, as if embarrassed. "A band coming up from Fort Randall?"

He'd phrased it as a question because our appearance there so suddenly made him think it wasn't true anymore; he wanted our understanding of their deep fear. Children were still crying, even though we were obviously threatening no one.

"You should all go home," I told them in Dutch and then in Frisian. "We have just come from a day's ride west of the river, and the whole place is calm." Eyes wide open, all over. I think the news was almost too much for them to take. "Give thanks to God," I said, "because what you've heard is simply not the truth. Everything will be fine. Give thanks to the Lord of heaven and earth."

Then Brinks turned to them and nodded, and at that they began to file out of the little church.

Later, when we were at the Brinks homestead—he invited us to stay the night—I asked him about the Balkema story. "You told me," I said, "that people wondered whether it wasn't Arie Boon who had something to do with Balkema's death. That the Indian story was an excuse. You said it yourself—lots of people thought so." We were sitting at the table with him and his wife, hot coffee all around.

He took a deep breath. "Sometimes fear can make fools of us all," he said. "With everything going on over there, it's easier to believe that the devil is working harder among the heathens. People are afraid, Jan—people believe strange things when they're afraid."

Brinks was right, of course, but I don't think even I understood at that moment how right he was. There is, after all, much more to this story you want me to tell you, much more.

When Dalitha and I left for Harrison the next morning, another long day's ride east to meet my parents, we knew more about the death of Dries Balkema. We knew that no one in Friesland knew much of anything about his trips across the Missouri, much less about a baby. Not once did Abraham Brinks mention anything about an Indian girl. Neither did we.

"Fordham is wrong. These people could not have been his killers," I said to Dalitha the next day when we were on our way to Harrison. And she knew I was right, because she'd heard more than enough of what they didn't know.

During the winter of 1881, when I lived in Hull, Iowa, and worked at the Verhey Wagon Shop, I felt much more alone than I ever did after moving west. My beloved Rinska had died two years earlier, in 1879. I'd buried her with our Jantje, the baby daughter who'd lived but a day before leaving this world in the single most torturous night of my life—the night on which we had expected such joy. Two years earlier, in '77, some mysterious sickness had taken our three-year-old Frederika and eight other children from the community where we'd built our home.

Our first daughter's death shook the foundations of my life, but Rinska's faith seemed an anchor when my own trust in God foundered. When I couldn't bring myself to read the Scriptures, Rinska would smile, lay her hand on mine, and do so herself, not self-righteously. She simply would not let me doubt God; she witnessed to his love by giving me hers.

And then she died. Putting her and Jantje in the sandy lakeshore soil was something I couldn't reconcile with the will of a loving God.

It has been the great blessing of my life to have loved two women and been loved by them—two women whose faith always surpassed mine, even though what it was they believed and how they practiced that faith seemed, at times, wholly different. And I say that because it is not possible for me to imagine myself farther from the love of God than I have been at times in my life; yet he has taken me back, always. Some people know that truth when they are children; some—most, I think—require a lifetime of instruction. I am one of those people.

Don't forget that when I tell you yet more of what you want to know.

In the winter of 1881 I told myself there was nothing for me in Hull, Iowa, or all of Sioux County, where people either lived by the upright moral codes of the community or spent their strength fighting them. Those were my choices. And that's why, for me, going to the Dakota Territory in April, 1882, seemed the right thing to do.

That Saturday when Dalitha and I drove into Harrison, South Dakota, eight years had passed since I'd come to that same place with dozens and dozens of others from Sioux County and found nothing on that flat grassland but an oyster can on a plaster lath to mark the goal of our journey—our newly claimed land. We got off the train in Plankington, unloaded the freight cars, hitched our horses to the wagons, bought lumber and provisions, and set out to build the new colony, a place someone called "New Orange" for a time, until it was renamed Harrison—after the president—which sounded far better because it was more American.

Eight years had passed, and Harrison now stood at the center of a wider community of almost three thousand Dutch people. I'd left the place in 1883, bound first for the western edge of the colony, Friesland. I'd been back to Harrison occasionally, but I had no roots in Douglas County really, and most of my freight was westbound.

Riding into town that morning was, for me, a shock. Where once I remembered nothing more than an oyster can, now a main street bustled with businesses—a barber shop, a newspaper office, a livery barn, a millinery shop, several dry goods stores, a machine shop, Frank LeCocq's bank, a hardware store, Fenenga Well Company, Den Beste Machinery, H. Vis Drug Store, and Jongewaard Meat Market—and not one but two hotels.

Dalitha was as struck by the growth of the town as I was, because she had guessed her arrival would be grist for the rumor mill the moment we rode into town together. But with the streets full of merchants and farm families in for supplies on a Saturday afternoon, we were, I think, almost unnoticed. She was no scandal on the streets of Harrison. No one paused to stare. People laughed, shouted across the street, raised caps to old friends, chatted on the wooden sidewalks, but the two

169

of us were unheralded as we pulled up to the Vander Linden Hotel.

It was a mark of my being more and more an American that we stayed in the hotel in Harrison. When I first married Dalitha, I had to be convinced that paying perfectly good money for a bed did not make me a shameless spendthrift, especially when there were perfectly good people in perfectly good homes to put us up for nothing at all. Not until I tied the horses to the rail in front of Harrison's finest hotel did I remember that. However, a bite of the old Dutch guilt did come back, and I quickly scanned the street to be sure no one I knew was watching when I marched into the lobby.

When I signed the ledger, the young man behind the desk, someone I didn't know, read my name and quickly started speaking in Dutch. "I don't understand," I told him, because he seemed the kind of boy it would be fun to tease.

His face went gray. "I'm sorry," he said, and he pointed at my name. "I just thought with your name . . ."

"We're not in Holland," I said reprovingly.

Dalitha jammed me so hard in the ribs that I almost burst into laughter, but then she crossed over in front of me and asked, with a straight face, "So where can we find the saloon?"

The boy could barely hide his embarrassment. "I'm afraid there are none in Harrison," he said, and Dalitha unloaded with a vulgar phrase I'd taught her in Dutch, something I won't repeat. The poor boy was completely confused. He didn't know where to look.

"I'm sorry," Dalitha said. "We're only joking with you."

That left him even more shocked.

"And what time is church tomorrow?" I asked. "My father is a dominie. I'm sure he will preach—at the *ware*," meaning the "true" Dutch Reformed church.

"Dominie Ellerbroek," he said, as if suddenly a burst of light had illuminated everything. He pointed at the ledger, where I'd signed. "From Rosebud?" he asked.

I pointed at Dalitha. "She runs a mission there, a teacher," I told him, and then I raised my hand as if covering my mouth and spoke to him in Dutch. I told him she had no idea what those naughty Dutch words meant— no idea.

He smiled as if he were suddenly part of the conspiracy. "Will you be having supper with us here?" he asked. "It will be served at six."

The plan was to meet my father and mother at the parsonage of the church later that evening. We'd said nothing about eating, so I told him we would be having our meal in the dining room. "Which is?" I said.

He pointed through a door to the left of the huge glass case he used as the front desk.

Dalitha went upstairs while I stepped back outside to retrieve our things and bring the wagon and horses to the livery. It was a most amazing thing. I spent some time on the main street of a village I had helped build less than a decade before. I must have seen dozens of people—

men and women, old folks and children—and not one of them could I claim to recognize, even though all of them, I'm sure, were Hollanders. The livery boy was toothless, I remember, and he loved my boots. He thought I was a cowboy from the Wild West.

"So when do I get my catechism training?" my wife said later when we were alone in our room.

I had no idea what she meant.

"You need to tell me how to behave here," she said.

"May as well tell the sun when to rise," I told her, and she took me in her arms.

We had supper in a small dining room—four or five tables. We were one of only two couples, and the fare was exceptionally good, mostly potatoes and beef roast with vegetables. It was, I admit, something of home, and more sumptuous than what I would have guessed a Harrison hotel could offer.

We dined in unexpected elegance that night, our food delivered by a woman in a perfectly white smock, her collars and sleeves crisply pressed. And the other couple—the ones who sat at the table opposite ours—seemed altogether from another world.

Prairie weather takes a toll on skin, especially around the face, where lines form quickly and seem permanent. Discoloration is common from too many seasons in the hot sun and the dusty winds. But this couple—middle-aged, we thought—seemed almost pampered, their faces soft and entirely unfit for life in Dakota. They spoke

172

reservedly to each other, I remember, which in itself was strange; perhaps when life is as difficult as it is where we live, the common bond between fellow travelers makes us all friends. But this couple—they seemed oblivious to us, a behavior we assumed was because they were rich, and we weren't.

Soon enough, we didn't even think about them. Soon enough, however, we would not be able to so simply disregard them.

A year before our trip to Harrison, Dalitha had met my father for the first time. After the long ride back to our reservation cabin, and after two days of near silence spent evaluating him, Dalitha finally said to me over a cup of coffee one night, "You know, Jan, you didn't have a father."

Dalitha is right about most things, but about that she was wrong.

When I was a boy, my mother told me more than once to hush my playing because my father was writing sermons. I remember that I never really spoke to him, even though he often spoke to me. I remember, at age ten or twelve, watching him in the pulpit and wondering how it was that I never saw that man at home—someone so expressive, so determined, so passionate in his preaching. My father was a man who gave his life to the church, and it never really occurred to me—not until Dalitha said what she did—that life could have been any different. What Dalitha didn't know was that my father also never wondered whether life could have or should have been different.

It is fair to say that sometime when I was a boy, I simply gave him up to his calling, presuming that the ministry of the Word and sacraments required all of him—heart, mind, soul, and strength. Which left, of course, very little for his children.

"Do you love him?" Dalitha said to me that night after I told her she was wrong.

Even then, twenty years after I'd left my father's house, I couldn't really answer that question because I didn't think it was fair.

A year later, in Harrison, on that Saturday night when we were going to meet them—my parents—my new wife and I walked three blocks east to the parsonage arm in arm in the cold night air. Dalitha knocked at the door, where we were received by the lady of the house, the *juffrouw*—Mrs. Vander Werp—then admitted into the hallway. It was dark, I remember, a single lamp on the wall behind us. A door to the front room on our left was closed, probably to save heat, since the open stairway to the second floor was directly to our right. It was necessary for us to walk up that long hallway, turn through the kitchen, then the dining room—it was a big house for Harrison—in order to enter what some Dutch people used to call the *mooie kamer,* the pretty room, suitable only for very special occasions. Then the lady of the house left us alone.

174

There my father sat, my mother beside him on the couch. He didn't rise because, I suppose, I was still and always would be the child. They both seemed pleased to see us, although my mother's smile was obviously a decoration—she had, after all, never met this woman I'd married somewhere far, far west of even the Mississippi River, and an American too. We shook hands, and my mother hugged me. And she hugged Dalitha, which surprised me. In fact, for a moment, my mother wouldn't let her go. Then she smiled, holding my wife's hands until both of us backed away slightly and waited for them to offer us a place to sit.

They spoke their best broken English. How were we doing? Wasn't the weather wonderfully warm? It was just as unseasonably warm in Michigan, although there had been already lots of snow. Your sister is fine (she lived with them, always had and always would). She sends her regards, wishes she could have come too, although she says she would have been afraid of coming so far to the middle of nowhere. Your brother has a church in the woods of northern Michigan. He and his wife and their children—all six—are all well, and sometimes they all come home to Noordeloos to visit.

And then a pause.

The papers are full of the treachery on the reservation, some strange dancing, Sitting Bull, Buffalo Bill, the threat of war, they said. It's hard for them to accept that their own son is actually out there because, after all, buffalo and blanketed Indians and their squaws and their papooses—

175

that whole thing seems so terribly savage and uncivilized, my mother said. And yes, of course, the local dominie is treating them well, offering hospitality that's almost as good as that which they receive in Grand Rapids, and fine Christian fellowship.

Nods all around.

"And *your* work?" my mother said to Dalitha.

"On the Rosebud, things seem almost ordinary," she told them. "Farther west the schools are completely empty right now."

It was a straightforward answer. I was happy Dalitha had decided to put on her best behavior.

"It must be a rich blessing," my mother said, "to know you are ministering in such need."

Dalitha nodded.

"You know," my mother said, "we always wanted Jan to be a preacher or a teacher."

"Every day he teaches me something," Dalitha told her, and then she winked. "And sometimes I get tired of his preaching."

And then my mother looked at my father as if he should take a lesson. That I remember.

"Are you considering a call?" I asked my father. It was still difficult for me to believe that they would come all the way across the country just to see me.

My mother looked down.

"You know, when first we came to America," my father said, "our church was a chicken coop." He laughed. "It is for young men to be in places like this, young men full of visions." He was referring to Harrison's preacher, Vander Werp, whom we had yet to meet. Then he looked around to be sure that what he was about to say wouldn't be repeated. "I don't know that your mother could live out here."

"And you could, I suppose?" she said.

I remember being surprised at how playful and open they seemed.

Then more small talk—a half hour or so. They wanted to know about my work, the long trips across the open prairie. They wanted to know about the Sioux—how were the missionaries doing? Was it true that the Indians painted their faces as hideously as the papers showed? And that screaming? Did we know about those boarding schools and the wonderful work they were doing out East? How long did we think it would take to turn the Sioux into good Christian farmers?

Some questions I answered quickly because I didn't want Dalitha to have the opportunity to say what I knew was on her mind.

Through all of that conversation, it was my mother who did most of the talking. That was not unusual—when I was growing up, it was simply assumed that my father would be too preoccupied by his high calling to focus on ordinary, day-to-day things. Besides, my mother prided herself on her old-country, upper-class origins and parenting. Sometimes I used to think that she regarded my choice of life on the reservation with an American woman to be not so much theologically questionable as, well,

177

unsavory for someone who could have and should have been an educated man, a dominie like his father—and his brother.

"You go to church?" my father said.

That was a serious question I seriously wanted to avoid. At the time, we were not what my father would call "faithful" church members, but then, of course, we didn't live in Harrison—and certainly not in Michigan. His own words came back to me. "In a chicken coop," I told him, which was, in part, the truth. "Maybe as big as this room, maybe a little bigger. Twelve or fifteen people—all Sioux—and the preacher, a fine man. Rev. Nobles, his name is."

"When I first came," Dalitha said, looking at my mother, "imagine my shock to worship with men dressed only in a breechcloth."

I'm sure my mother was not capable even of imagining something so outrageously indecorous. "And still?" she asked.

"All of them wear white clothes now," Dalitha told them. "From the government. Those days are over."

I don't know exactly why—maybe it was the fact that their openness seemed so new to me—but for whatever reason, I said, "You should come." I meant it. "You're this far, Mother; you and Father should come back with us. It's only two days' travel."

And that's when the truth finally came out. "We haven't come simply to visit, Jan," my father said. "We are here to see you, that's true, but we have reason to believe that

178

you—that both of you—can be of help to good Christian people we know." He reached into his vest and pulled out his watch, as if expecting something to happen. "There are people with us here in Harrison—fine people, up-standing believers—who want very much to speak with you about the sadness in their souls. They want to speak to you, both of you."

"That's why you're here?" I said.

"On my salary, Jan, it would be impossible to take such a trip." He looked at my mother. "These people—I am expecting them any minute—they have the means."

My father looked at his watch; my mother glanced up at the cuckoo clock on the wall, and at that moment the sound of boots on the porch interrupted the silence. They were Dutch, so I should have known they'd be on time.

It was the people we'd seen in the dining room at the hotel just three blocks away, and they were the parents of a young man named Andries Balkema who'd been alone in Dakota and who'd been shot and killed on a homestead somewhere west of Harrison.

You can only imagine our shock. Dalitha was speech-less, as was I.

From what we'd seen of them in the dining room at the hotel, we'd guessed they were rich. What we hadn't seen, however, was something I noticed in the man the moment he sat down in the chair beside my father and began to speak—that he was not a man unaccustomed to work. His shoulders were broad, his hands square and calloused. And it was not easy for him to explain what he felt he had to—not simply because what he wanted to tell us involved something hard to talk about, but also because it wasn't that easy for him to speak. His wife found the task no easier.

People who speak well use their hands because they're not afraid. Those who are afraid leave their hands in their pockets. I learned that from the Sioux, who never use their hands until they know you well. Adriaan Balkema did not use his hands, not at all.

I am reminded of Joseph of Egypt when I tell you this part of the story. Mr. and Mrs. Balkema knew nothing of what we knew about their son and his young woman from the reservation. Of course, we knew nothing of what they knew, so for a time all we could do was listen and watch them suffer as they haltingly explained to us what little they knew about the tragedy of their son's death and what they thought to be its cause. What they told us, however, included his having intimate relations with an Indian girl outside of the marriage vows, which would have been hard to discuss even if she were a girl from the church.

The memory of Balkema trying to tell us everything is still painful to me, as it was then. Soon I had no doubt why my father and mother consented to come with them all the way from Michigan. The Balkemas wanted my father and mother beside them in their hour of need, even though they were not members of my father's congregation. Noordeloos was my father's church. The Balkemas were in Grand Rapids, at East Street, but their dominie knew my father had a son on the reservation.

"It seems the Indians killed him," Balkema told me, his eyes lowered, "perhaps in revenge or jealousy for his sin with the young woman."

He spoke to me, not to Dalitha, although he rarely raised his eyes. For a long time his wife sat in silence. He reached in his pocket. "In his things," he said—he was speaking English, not Dutch—"in his things we found this note." He got up slowly from the chair in which he was sitting—he was a big man, I remember, strong—and handed me the note. Dalitha and I were sitting across the room on dining room chairs that the preacher's wife had brought in after the Balkemas had arrived. I scanned it quickly; it was a letter Dries had never sent to Anna Crow. Dalitha pulled at my arm, and I leaned toward her so she too could read.

The note too was painful. Mrs. Balkema had a hanky knotted in her hand the whole time they were there. At first, I don't remember her speaking, but I remember her eyes.

Anna Crow had ended the relationship, not Dries Balkema. That seemed clear. He begged her to let him see her again. His desperation made it obvious that she must have left little doubt about his taking more trips across the Mud on Nick Fordham's ferry. And then this—the only line I remember: "This baby of ours will also be, you know, my child."

181

Balkema spoke again. "Somewhere close, we think, there is an Indian girl named Anna who is with child— and that child belongs, in part, to us."

That's what he had come to say, all the way from Michigan, my own parents with him—with them—I suppose in a way to buoy their spirits and hopes.

"You believe we can find her?" I said.

"We know of no other means," he said. "We hoped you might help."

It was difficult to dislike these people—they'd come directly to the point, and they didn't swagger or patronize, the way Easterners often can. They were more wealthy than anyone I believe I have ever spoken to in my life, but they didn't seem proud.

"The promise is to the children, to the third and fourth generation thereof," he said laboriously, but not as if quoting from Scripture should mark the end of the conversation. "We believe that this child—our son's son or daughter—is still a child of the covenant."

I was raised in a preacher's home, and I knew that language. I knew what was behind the words, because I was also a child of the covenant, and I knew my own parents would have argued the same theology in their concern for a son who had walked away from the church at the death of his wife and children.

"You want us to find this girl?" Dalitha said.

"We would like to have the child," Balkema said.

"And not the mother?" she asked quickly.

182

Balkema looked at his wife for the first time, not because he expected an answer from her but because I don't think he really knew how to answer the question himself.

"She's an Indian," my mother said.

There was so much to fear. I knew it would take every bit of Dalitha's strength to fight the impulse that she felt.

"I know she's an Indian," Dalitha said, "but I mean, do you know anything else about this young girl?"

They did not, of course. Not one of the four of them had considered that there might be a need to say something further. This Anna was, after all, a savage. The Balkemas were rich and believers, among the elect, to be sure. It was beyond them to even guess there should be reason to know anything more about the situation than those obvious—and eternal—differences.

"Can you find this woman?" Balkema said. "We are here to ask you that question."

I waited, wondering if Dalitha would speak, but she told me later that she didn't talk at first because this was my fight, because these were my people. There I sat, like Joseph with his brothers in Egypt, knowing so much but not knowing exactly how it all could be told.

"How did you get the note?" I asked.

"The man for whom he worked," Balkema told me. "He sent his things, what little he had. In the Bible we gave him when he was a boy—in the Bible," he pointed at the paper in my hand, "that letter."

"The man—his name?" I said.

"Boon, Arie Boon."

"And nothing more?" I said.

Balkema was looking at me now, relieved perhaps, because the burden had been laid upon us.

"There was no more to the story than what you found in your son's things?" I asked again.

Balkema shook his head, then nodded toward his wife, who shook her head.

"There were no jobs in Michigan?" I asked. "Why was he here?"

Then his hands were in front of him, where he folded and unfolded them rapidly, nervously. "He wanted no part of home," Balkema said, and he kept looking at his wife as if he were uncomfortable doing all the talking and wanted her to help him.

"He could find no work?" I asked.

Down went the eyes.

It was not a joy to play with him or his feelings—their feelings—but I wanted to know him, and their son; and I knew Dalitha would want to know everything too. After all, they were asking for a child about whom they knew nothing. I wanted to see what kind of parents they were and had been.

"My son could have worked for me," Balkema said. "My men and I build houses. We build many houses on the east side of the city."

"And he was way out here?" Dalitha said.

Then Mrs. Balkema finally spoke. Balkema looked at his wife, not as if to give her permission but to acknowl-

184

edge that there were some things she could say better than he could. "Since he is gone," she said, "we have had to carry the burden of knowing that maybe we pushed him too hard."

"Work?" I said.

"Jan," Mr. Balkema said, "when I came to this country, I had nothing—we had nothing. What did I know but work? But our children, today they grow up in a different world." I think he sensed somehow that Dalitha would be the toughest to convince, because he looked directly at her when he said what he did next. "I don't know why or how my son died," he said, "but I know this—it was in part because his father did not love him in the way of the Word."

His wife stood and came to his chair, and when she put her hand on his shoulder he leaned his head against her side.

There was little pleasure in watching the pain of those parents. I have come to believe that forgiveness is the most difficult thing we can ever do, but in the presence of such contrite hearts as we saw that night, it was impossible, at least for me, not to want to give to them exactly what it was they were looking so hard to find. The Balkemas had been blessed with wealth beyond any Hollanders I'd ever known, but I believe they would have given every dollar they had in return for their son.

Still, it seemed to me that for us to tell them everything we knew about Anna Crow right then—how she'd taken up with the dancers, how she wouldn't listen to anything we'd said, how angry she was with *washechu,* how at that very moment we were afraid for her life—telling them that would have, I think, only deepened their grief and hurt.

I sat there at a loss for words. I looked at Dalitha, but this was not a time in which she was going to lead. She reached for my hand, and when she did, I knew she was telling me that I had to tell them something.

"Her name is Anna Crow," I said.

"You know?" Balkema asked, shocked.

"We know," I said. "She has been for several years at a boarding school out East."

"Thank God," Mrs. Balkema said.

I reached for Dalitha's hand because I didn't want her saying what I knew was right there on her lips.

"That experience," I said, "it has made her into something she never expected, something half-Sioux and half-white."

"She must have loving parents," my father said. He didn't understand; I don't think any of them did.

"She does," I told him. "Her father is Broken Antler, her mother is called Rises with the Sun. We know them. You should know that they are just as worried."

"She's not with them?" Mrs. Balkema asked.

I looked at Dalitha.

"What is it?" my mother said.

Dalitha pinched my hand hard. "I think you and me," she told me, "we need to speak alone together." She kept hold of my hand and stood, then tipped her head toward the front porch of the parsonage. We had to walk back through the room, in front of them—my parents and the Balkemas—but Dalitha was right. The two of us had to talk.

Outside, I remember shivering, feeling very cold. Dalitha was shivering too. It was December after all, and clear. A cloudless night, even when the day is warm, can be cold as winter. But it wasn't the cold that made me shiver. It was fear, not knowing what to say, what to do, what was right.

"You know I could weep for them," Dalitha told me. "Their sadness is not something put on, Jan. I don't know your people, but I know grief and hurt when I see it, and they have more than enough to bear."

I knew she had more to say.

"But they hate Indians," she said. She stepped off the porch because she didn't want them to hear anything inside.

"Hate?" I said.

"You heard me. It never crossed their minds that that child could have a good life on the Rosebud. It never dawned on them."

"They're rich," I said.

"And look what happened to this boy of theirs, Dries."

"They're broken. You said it yourself."

She looked fiercely into my eyes. "You know why they want that child, Jan," she said. "They think that child's life will be worthless on the reservation. He'll turn into some drunk—that's what they think."

187

"And you're sure he won't?" I said.

"Maybe it's a girl—she'll become a fat old drunken half-blood."

Dalitha was right, of course.

"They say it's a covenant child," I told her. She had no idea what that meant. "They think somewhere in its heart there's God's own promise to believers."

"They think it's *theirs,* that's what they're saying. They think the baby is *theirs,* Jan, and you know it."

"And it isn't?" I said. "Besides, what they mean is that the child belongs to God."

"Nonsense," she said. "They mean it belongs to them somehow. Besides, if it belongs to God, then God will do with this baby what he will."

"Is that right?" I said. "That's very strange theology, coming from you."

"Theology," she said. "What has all of this to do with theology? You know Broken Antler, you know Rises with the Sun. Is there nothing of them in this child? And ask yourself this: How many Sioux children will she know when she grows up in the fancy parlor of rich white people who build houses in the city? How many brown faces will she count among her friends?"

"Ask yourself this," I said. "If we say no, how often will she go to bed hungry, this little girl? And what on earth will happen to her parents when all of this messiah madness goes up in smoke? Will they build her a home? The buffalo are gone, Dalitha. What's really left for them there?" And I pointed west.

188

"You're one of them," she told me, pointing back inside. "You're no better than they are."

Only a few times in our marriage did the two of us stand so close yet seem so far away. But when I remember that moment now, I know this too—that we were, each of us, straining at arguments for the sake of truth. Dalitha wasn't wrong, and neither was I, even though what ran between us seemed wider than the Mud come spring.

I feared reservation life back then far more than Dalitha did. She was right—I still was one of the Dutch in some ways. But to snatch the child from Anna Crow, from Broken Antler and Rises with the Sun—that would have been something I couldn't do, despite my fears. To do that required me to believe that Anna Crow didn't matter, that her whole life had no meaning, that she was merely the human body that was to give birth to a child who was worth so much more. To do what they wanted required me to believe that nothing at all mattered but the Balkemas' will, even though they would have said, I'm sure, that what they wanted was surely God's own desire for the child. They were not pushy, they were not proud, they were not demanding. But I knew very well they were not right either, despite their firm confidence in the biblical principle they were using to try to rescue their grandchild.

Dalitha was right, and I told her so. It wasn't because I agreed with her all the way here, but because I realized—we both did, really—that the plan of the Balkemas took no consideration for the fact that Anna Crow too was created in the image of God. "You're right," I said, "we simply cannot do what they want."

Dalitha turned—we were maybe fifty feet from the porch, both of us shivering with the stars shining above us—and she looked at me strangely, almost as if she didn't trust me.

"We can't do it," I said. "We won't do it, but what do we tell them?"

"The truth," she said. I remember the steam coming from her lips. "Tell them the truth, Jan."

"It will only make them more desperate," I said, because people of means like the Balkemas could buy favors all the way up and down the river. "They can hire out men who don't care one bit about Anna Crow," I told her. "They can hire out men who will kill. They have the means."

"Not them," she said, pointing back inside. "Not these people. They won't do it. They have contrite hearts."

"Must we tell them everything?" I said. "The Ghost Dance?"

"You heard them—they read the papers," she said.

"And then what?"

She didn't know what I meant.

"And then we hope for the best?" I asked.

"You mean for them?"

"I mean for this child," I told her. "How do we know what will happen to this child?"

"Isn't faith the sure knowledge of things hoped for?"

That's exactly what she said, quoting Scripture.

190

When we came back into the house and walked up the hallway through the kitchen, the preacher's wife offered two hot cups of coffee. Once more we walked in front of them all—my mother, my father, and the Balkemas, who were now sitting together on the couch next to my parents. The two of us took our wooden dining chairs in front of a wall of books.

"He loved her, your son," I told them. "We found out as much when we were coming here from a man who runs the ferry across the Missouri. Mr. Fordham remembers him coming back from the reservation." I'm not sure why I started there, but I did. "I found it good to learn that," I told them. "Maybe that's why I'm telling you now. He loved her."

"I don't understand," my mother said. My mother was raised in Amsterdam. She had given me a childhood full of books and was determined not to let me or my brother and sister become one of these *boers* she felt surrounded by in the Dutch community. She had no idea how a child of the Balkemas could fall in love with a savage. "He loved her?" she said.

"As a man loves a woman," I told her, my own American wife beside me, "and a woman loves a man. And she is *in verwachting*," I told them. "That we think we know."

"And where does she live?" Mrs. Balkema said. "We will go there. We will meet this woman ourselves if she loves our—if our son loved her."

"You can take us," Balkema said. "I will hire you. It's what you do for a living, your father says."

191

The truth, Dalitha had said—they needed to know the truth.

"We don't know where she is," I told them, because that was the truth. We had no idea, right then, and we certainly could not have guessed. "What we know about Anna Crow is that she's left the school where she was teaching and has taken up with the dancers—the Ghost Dancers." Not the least bit of recognition appeared in their eyes. I looked at my father, who also had little idea what I was talking about. "In the newspapers," I said. "You've not read about it?"

None of them knew.

"It's a delusion," Dalitha said, "a false religion, and once the snow comes, it will disappear into thin air, I'm sure."

At that point I think they knew we feared telling them the whole truth.

"The Ghost Dancers?" my father said. "What kind of false religion is this?"

I explained about Wovoka, about Short Bull and Kicking Bear having gone to Nevada to meet him, about the ceremonies, about men and women dancing into a frenzy, about visions of returning buffalo, of the old ones reappearing, of white people being swept away by floods, of the Indian inheriting a new, green earth. And then I told them what I thought would be the most difficult part—how Jesus Christ had appeared and told them all of this would happen. "Jesus Christ has heard their groanings, they say. He knows their suffering, and he's coming again, this time for them. And that is why they dance."

192

No one spoke a word.

"People call it 'the messiah craze,'" I said. "We thought maybe you knew."

"With their hearts they believe this?" my father said.

"Deeply," Dalitha said. "It is what Anna Crow believes."

"Even in Jesus Christ?" my father asked.

"Some of them claim to see his pierced hands and side, when they have the vision," I told them.

"And he is coming for them?" Mrs. Balkema said.

"Only for them," her husband told her.

Their reaction surprised Dalitha and even softened her. Most of the people we knew back then thought of the messiah craze as merely delusion, a kind of hysteria caused by starvation and the death of the Sioux way of life—and it was. But what Dalitha saw in my parents and in the Balkemas was a kind of grudging respect even for beliefs they didn't share but could somehow understand, being deeply religious themselves.

Mrs. Balkema, I remember, covered her eyes with her hands.

"It will pass with winter?" my father said to Dalitha.

"When spring comes and we're still here," she said, gesturing toward me and toward them, "then it will become clear that what they believed was not the truth."

"And what then?" my father said. "Who will be there to mend their souls?"

"Only God can mend their souls," Dalitha said.

What the Balkemas must have imagined right then about a woman they didn't know, the young woman carrying their grandchild, were the gray eyes of despair ravaged by the worst kind of pain, the tearing up of the soul. "We must find her," Mrs. Balkema said. "You must help us. For her sake too. For the girl's sake, this Anna Crow. You must find her and bring her out of that madness."

"It's very dangerous," Dalitha said.

"For her?" Mr. Balkema asked.

"For her," Dalitha told him, "and for us. The whole reservation is dangerous. The military has taken control away from the agents, and the military rules with an iron fist. The people are afraid too—the Sioux."

"Some Indians have far less faith than anger," I told them, because Dalitha would not have.

"Will there be fighting?" my father asked.

"We have taken all their land, never once fulfilled a promise, robbed them of their buffalo, and given them a pittance," Dalitha said. "And all around them they see more and more white people every day. Is it any wonder that they are angry? They have no food. No one grew anything this year—no one." Then she looked directly at my father. "Ask your son," she said. "Not so long ago he held a dead baby in his own hands."

Dalitha didn't understand what the picture she'd painted did within the minds of both of my parents and myself, because I once had held my own dead child in my arms in their presence. In a moment, the three of us were back in the lakeshore woods at a funeral from which I'd walked west and never returned. I didn't look away from my father's eyes, even though I knew that what he

194

was searching for in mine right then was nothing about a woman named Anna Crow but instead something about his son.

"She is too?" Mrs. Balkema said. "This girl—Anna Crow—she is starving and angry?"

"She is one of them," Dalitha said.

"Then you must help us for sure," she said. "You have to find her and remove her from that danger. She will have our child."

"Does not the Lord himself search the mountaintops for the lost sheep?" Mr. Balkema said. "He says in his Word that he cares more for the one than the ninety-and-nine, Dominie." He looked at my father. "He cares more about the one who is lost from the fold. Is that not so?"

My mother understood. But no one else in that room knew what didn't need to be said between my father and me right then. And here's what I saw when Balkema asked him a question that was, at that moment, as much about me as it was about Anna Crow. I saw something soft in my father's eyes, softer than anything I'd seen on the day when my wife and my baby daughter were put into the ground. For the first time, I saw something less than sure confidence in him, something less than a firm conviction, and something more of love.

"You must help us," Mrs. Balkema said again. "It is not only her soul at stake here, but it is the soul of our grandchild. Our son is already gone. We won't let our grandchild slip away."

"You want us to drag her out of there?" Dalitha said. "You want us to wrap her hands and tie her legs and bring her here to Harrison?"

"It's her soul here, that's what is at stake, don't you see?" Mrs. Balkema said. "As soldiers of the King, you must help us."

That's when I told them the whole story—how we had chased her as far west as Pine Ridge; how she was with a man, a fine young man named Wolves in Camp, who obviously cared for her; how her hair was growing out; how the look on her face seemed full of peace; how she believed that Jesus Christ was coming for the Sioux. And then we told them more—about the lines of troops digging into the ground as if expecting battle.

"Even you are afraid?" Mrs. Balkema said.

"Yes, we're scared," I said.

"Then you must find her."

"Even if we could," I told her, "it would be wrong. Anna Crow is, like us, a human being. She must find her own way." At that moment I didn't look at my father.

"She is with them—the dancers," Mrs. Balkema said. "Her life is in danger, and the life of her child. You said it yourselves. You must go and bring her back."

"What God wants is our love," I said, and I looked directly at my father. "We cannot make her a prisoner to us or the Christian faith. What God wants is her will, just as he wants yours and mine." And then I turned to my father, the dominie, because I wanted to hear him. I wanted to know what he would say to his own wayward son. "What he wants is our will, isn't that right, Father?"

"Tell them what they must do, Dominie," Mr. Balkema said.

My father looked first at me for what seemed a long time, as if he were judging; then he turned to the Balkemas, the people whose cause he'd come all the way to South Dakota to present. "My son is right," he said. "We cannot bind this girl's faith, nor imprison her against her will. What God wants from us, from each of us, is that we give him what we are, freely."

For the Balkemas, I'm sure, something was broken at that moment. But for me, there is no question but that something was healed.

# ⊰ *Nine* ⊱

It was my idea not to attend worship on Sunday and instead to start home, even though we'd planned to stay in Harrison and be near my parents until Monday.

When we left the parsonage on Saturday night, we walked away from grieving people who would, soon enough, come to occupy the room beside ours in the Vander Linden Hotel. That night, their proximity kept me awake, along with my fretfulness about what the Balkemas had wanted us to do. There was no question in my mind that Dalitha and I could not go out to hunt down Anna Crow and drag her back like some runaway slave; but I'd also seen burning grief in the faces of two people whose sadness convinced me they had suffered a great deal—and whose eyes made it clear they didn't understand why we couldn't cooperate with the plan they'd come all the way to South Dakota to carry out. Our decision was the right one, but I wasn't happy.

It was Dalitha who said that to leave without saying good-bye to my parents would be wrong, so, aboard the wagon, with the sun only beginning to climb above the flat land east of town, we rolled up in front of the parsonage to tell them we wouldn't be staying, that we'd miss church because our journey west simply could not wait.

I dare say I was the only Hollander in Harrison that morning not dressed in his Sunday best, but we had miles to go and the dust was terrible. Through the window in the front door, I saw the preacher's wife standing at the stove, getting breakfast. I knew my father would already be dressed in his swallowtail coat. It was, after all, the Sabbath.

Dalitha did the talking when the preacher's wife came to the door. She told her there were these concerns back home, and we had thought we would have time to stay longer, but since we faced a long trip and, well, things being the way they were on the reservation, it was simply best that we leave immediately. The preacher's wife looked at me as if to make sure it wasn't some godless American plot to keep us away from Sabbath worship.

Then came my mother—she'd heard Dalitha's voice—and then my father. The preacher's wife withdrew, and the four of us stood on the front porch in the cold morning air. Dalitha repeated what she'd just said, and my mother smiled then reached for my wife's hands. Once again, somewhat surprisingly, she embraced her, and then me, as if she understood.

"There's an ox in the ditch, Father," I said, referring to Scripture.

He put a hand to his ear mockingly, as if he'd heard nothing, then nodded as if he'd understood. "These Balkemas," he said, "all the way from Michigan we've been with them on the train. They're fine Christian people. It will be hard for them."

I told him we would do what we could.

Then he reached for Dalitha. "You're a strong woman, like his mother," he said, nodding toward her. He took Dalitha's hand and drew her quickly to himself, as my mother had done, held her, patted her back. I was amazed.

"They're people, Dominie—the Sioux," my wife said. "Their tears rise from broken hearts that beat the same as ours."

"They don't know the Lord," he told her, letting her go.

"Same as here," she said, meaning Harrison. "Some do, some don't."

"And this mother, this Anna Crow?" he said.

"Anna Crow is like many of us," she said. "Confused."

And then he turned to me. "'Like many of us,'" he repeated, looking straight into my eyes.

"Not so confused as you think, maybe," I told him, and I reached for his hand because I'd not forgotten what he'd done the night before, how he'd stood with me, despite the heartrending sadness of the Balkemas. He embraced me, and with his right hand on my shoulder and his left hand holding Dalitha's, he prayed—for us, for the Balkemas, for Anna Crow, and for the baby yet to be born. My mother once more held Dalitha, and then we left.

There may have been a time in those dark moments when Rinska and our baby died that my father held me the way he did just for a moment on the parsonage porch that Sunday morning, but I don't remember it. And my not remembering is, I suppose, a part of my anger back then, both at him and the God he so dutifully served. But that morning, even though Dalitha and I were breaking the Sabbath by journeying back across the Missouri when we should have been resting, even though we were deliberately absenting ourselves from the fellowship of the saints, even though we were leaving them behind, that morning my father embraced me the way I had wanted him to years before.

That's what I remember, because I didn't expect it and because I never saw my father again. He never returned to South Dakota, and in just a few short years, the Lord took him home.

The night we returned, the 15th of December, no later than 8:00, Rises with the Sun rode up to our cabin in the darkness and told us what had occurred on the Standing Rock reservation. Sitting Bull was dead, she said, killed by *ceska maza,* the "metal chests," specially selected Sioux braves deputized as agency police.

That night, we learned very little about what happened at the great chief's camp on the Grand River, a hundred miles or more from where we lived, but since that time

I've heard the story. For whatever reason—religious or political—Sitting Bull made it clear to the agency and the army that he wanted to travel to Pine Ridge because the messiah would appear there—that's what he told them. Short Bull and Kicking Bear were already in camp in a place called "the stronghold," a secluded place in the Badlands where the bluecoats could not get at them and their followers. That's where he wanted to go, he said, to dance. Agent McLaughlin, whom Dalitha admired and many Sioux respected, wouldn't let him go.

So a company of almost fifty deputized Sioux rode into Sitting Bull's camp early in the morning, pulled him out of bed, and tried—even though they were quickly surrounded by a crowd of his family and supporters—to get old Bull on a horse and on his way to Fort Yates. In such a situation, there's dry grass and fire and then wind. Things flash into flame. Soon enough, the old hero was dead, not at the hands of a *washechu* but one of his own, a man named Red Tomahawk, who shot him in the back of the head when he saw the leader of the *ceska maza,* Sgt. Bull Head, go down when he took a bullet from one of Sitting Bull's band.

I don't know what you know of all of this—who shot who and why and who lived and who died. It may be a story you've heard often where you live, and it may be foolish to walk through those actions as if they could somehow be replayed in exactness. But when the dust finally cleared—and there was much dust—when finally the bluecoats arrived at Sitting Bull's camp, they found

202

eight dead Sioux from the camp of the old chief, along with two dead horses. Inside Sitting Bull's cabin, where the *ceska maza* had holed up, there were four dead policemen and three wounded, two of whom would die later. What little was left of peace was now bloodied and broken.

What Rises with the Sun could not tell us was a bit of news that didn't rank with the impact of the death of the great Sitting Bull. One of the most faithful of the dancers, a young man named Crow Woman, had, aboard his jet black pony, deliberately made three dangerous passes in front of the *ceska maza* holed up in Sitting Bull's cabin after the carnage. Wielding only a lance, he'd made himself a target, singing these words: "Father, I thought you said we were going to live."

Even though the attackers all fired at Crow Woman as he passed in front of them, miraculously he rode out of the valley of the camp. Untouched and triumphant.

Crow Woman was wearing a red ghost shirt, and his triumph proved to him and the others who had witnessed the miracle that Kicking Bear was right when he said that wearing the holy shirts would make Sioux braves invulnerable. They need not fear the bullets of the bluecoats or the *ceska maza*. Such miraculous faith doesn't need the wind to spread quickly.

Rises with the Sun hadn't heard that story, so neither did we—not then at least, and not for years afterward. But those who witnessed Crow Woman's apparent invincibility, and those who heard the story, were strengthened in their faith in the new messiah and the things he would bring, the things they'd hoped for.

I have told you before that Sitting Bull was no favorite of Dalitha, perhaps because she thought he didn't take his calling as chief and holy man as seriously as she thought he should. Whatever the reason, his death did not sadden her, although she was furious that the military had somehow arranged that Sitting Bull's blood would be on the hands of his own people, as was the blood of Crazy Horse before him. What saddened her was that his death meant things were now well out of control all over the reservations. She kept praying for cold weather, for blizzards, the kind that stop every movement on the plains, like the one in which we'd fallen in love. But no blizzard came, and when Christmas arrived a week or so later, the dusky prairie grasses still crackled in the wind, more October-like than mid-winter.

The chicken coop church I told my father we sometimes attended was presided over by a man named the Reverend Mr. Andersen Nobles, a Congregational preacher—very dedicated and humble. Sometimes I used to wonder what my father would preach if he were placed in such a church in the middle of nowhere, two white faces in the congregation and maybe two dozen brown. I wondered what his version of the gospel would sound like out here, where few of his parishioners would have ever been to school and none of them would have ever heard of Holland or a seminary in a place called Kampen. What would have really counted from all that training and all those years of vigorous theology, out here in the open sky on the limitless land?

For a long time now I have been telling you the story you wanted to know. It has come back to me because it has never left, although in piecing it together for you, this story has taught me things I didn't think I knew. Now we are coming to the end, but before we get there, I want to tell you about that Christmas in the little church in the middle of a storm far worse than any blizzard South Dakota ever saw. I want to tell you who was there. I hope that you will listen.

A woman whose name I remember as Red Feather was one of us that Christmas night. In famine and poverty, it is the children who suffer the most, and Red Feather, earlier in the fall, had lost a boy not yet a year old. She considered herself a Christian woman and faithfully attended Nobles's little church, alone. I never met her husband. Most often her three older children would come with her, although in their teenage years we saw little of them. What I remember about her is her persistence at the burial of that baby.

To balance the claims of the new Christian faith with the duties of the old ways was difficult, even for a man like Rev. Nobles, who was not a demanding soul. He wouldn't abide certain rituals that seemed to him too much like pagan superstitions. But at the burial of her baby, Red Feather badly wanted to put a favorite rattle in her child's casket. That was all she asked. As devoted a believer as she was, she could not discard all of the old ways. When Nobles assented, she put the rattle in the coffin with the body, and I will never forget the joy on her face.

Jackson Trombeau sat in the back, I remember. When his brother-in-law died, his wife's sister became his second wife, by tribal tradition. She was young and beautiful, and he was more than happy to have her in his cabin. She, however, was not happy to be there. More than once she left him. So he brought her to Nobles and asked to have her baptized—and Nobles knew why. Trombeau assumed that if his new wife were baptized, the church would keep her locked up at home. It was a request that Nobles refused. He wasn't about to bestow the sacrament as if it were a ball and chain. Jackson Trombeau and his first wife celebrated Christmas with us that night in December, 1890.

Lucy Spotted Horses was there with her husband. Sometime during the first summer after Dalitha and I were married, she'd come to our house late at night in tears because, she said, her husband had hit her and she'd left him. Later that night, Dalitha woke me up when she heard hushed voices outside our cabin. Lucy's husband had come. I remember Dalitha's hand on mine; I think she assumed I would have to run him off. For a long time, they talked. We could hear the soft tones of their discussion—it was not angry. In the morning, Lucy was gone, her blanket folded neatly where she'd been lying on the floor. I don't know whether he ever hit her again, but I remember the two of them in church that Christmas night.

206

There was another woman there, white, so cocksure of her every opinion, so confident of her sense of right and wrong that dealing with her was somewhat akin to dealing with a windy prairie fire. She was not a habitual pray-er but someone, maybe, like King David, who used to command the Lord to listen simply to the sound of his groaning. Those prayers, the wordless ones, were her strength. She never cared much at all for the duties of the Christian faith—church attendance and such. With her own brand of blessed arrogance, she believed that her life was her worship. I don't know that she would have made a good member of the Harrison church, but I loved her. She was my wife. She was there.

Beside her sat a man who'd more than once looked up into the open sky above the Michigan lakeshore woods, gazed at a hundred thousand stars, and wondered whether there really was some unimaginable realm named heaven, with Jehovah as its ruler. That stubborn doubt and the anger that caused it stayed with him for years, even when the sky opened broadly, endlessly, above the yawning plains where he'd come to live. There sat a man who'd lost his ability to trust in a God he'd never doubted until so much of what he'd loved had vanished.

That white man, that night, sat beside that white woman who never doubted her own vision of God's will. An odd pair, but very much in love.

I have told you about some of the people who worshipped that night, Christmas, in the chicken coop church—some of the people who may well have felt, as

I did, that where we were gathered just then was not altogether different from a little barn in Bethlehem. I'm telling you this because I want you to know that when he says, "Come unto me, all you who labor and are heavy-burdened," this Savior means what he says. It is not for the strong that he came to earth, but for us, the weak, the human. Excuse me for my preaching.

The stars appreciate winter because their radiance grows more fierce in the cold. When Dalitha and I rode home that night in our wagon, the heavens spilled a million diamonds.

"What must it have been like to see the star of Christmas?" Dalitha said. We were bundled tight and warm against the cold air, but in the moon's bright light the prairie shone like glass. "Just think—to look up into this sky and see, suddenly, something so huge and bright and never seen before," she said.

"No wonder they followed it."

"It's all so small, you know," she said, "the manger, the barn, the inn is full, the straw, the cows, all of that at the birth of a Savior." And then she pointed. "Except the heavens," she said, still looking up. "In Bethlehem it was something no one noticed—some poor people and a baby that should not have been there. But up there, it was written huge in the sky."

I half expected a comet right then.

"You know, Jan, it was as if God couldn't help himself. Somewhere he had to paint it large."

That was a moment of love in a long story that's not yet over. There's more to tell, and more yet to come while the Lord tarries.

Christmas, 1890. I remember the light in Rev. Nobles's little church, the shining land beneath the dazzling sky, and the peace we felt right then, because there was, at that moment, so very little.

We knew nothing of the whereabouts of Anna Crow. Heavy with child, she and Wolves in Camp were resting after an all-night march south toward Pine Ridge with the band of a fine man named Big Foot. Tired, weary, and very hungry, they made camp on that very Christmas Eve on the White River. None of them—nor us—had any idea what horrors were yet to befall them.

On the day after Christmas, in the morning, a young man came to our door with the news that Rises with the Sun had gone north toward Standing Rock because Broken Antler, her husband, had urged her to join him. She started out on Christmas Day in the company of a man who said he would protect her, and she'd left word that Sister Ward should be told of her going.

It was a boy, one of Dalitha's students, who brought the news. I remember coming to the door and seeing him there, scared to death of me, a white man he didn't know. "Sister Ward?" he said. He had a small hat in his hands.

Dalitha was behind me. "Charley?" she said. Some of her students made a habit of visiting our cabin, but this boy was not one I'd seen before.

209

He spoke in the Sioux language. I had no idea what he was saying, but I could see the fear that appeared on my wife's face. He repeated what he'd been assigned to say to her, that Rises with the Sun had gone on Christmas Day to the north somewhere, where she thought she would find her daughter. Broken Antler had found Anna and had sent word across the reservation that he wanted his wife—Anna's mother—to come. She had complied.

"Where?" Dalitha asked the boy.

He said he'd been told that the stragglers who had left Sitting Bull's camp had joined with a band of Minneconjou Sioux, Big Foot's band, and were moving south near the White River, much closer to us than we had imagined. Then he told her something that caused her to turn and stare at me. "He says Wolves in Camp is a brother of Sitting Bull," she said.

"Brother?" I was shocked.

"He means a relative," she told me. She reached for the boy's head and pushed his hair gently behind his ear, then said something to him in the Sioux language that was reassuring, because soon, for the first time, he smiled, nodded, and bowed, in the white way, in the way someone must have told him to address white people.

We had every reason to admire Wolves in Camp—he'd been nothing but gracious and even helpful in every moment we'd been with him. He was honest, and it was obvious that he cared for Anna Crow. But what scared Dalitha was that the old ways were never really dead, and for reasons that had less to do with his desire than his character, Wolves in Camp might well feel that to avenge the death of his great uncle or to die doing it was a matter of personal honor and homage.

"We must go," Dalitha told me, because she thought it was our calling to help a young woman who seemed deeply committed to not wanting our help. It was not the baby that my wife wanted, it was the baby's mother. What Dalitha knew—and what she needed to explain to me—was that Sitting Bull's murder, most likely in the presence of Wolves in Camp, was something that might make him want to act in ways that would put Anna Crow's life in real danger.

That we had promised my parents and the Balkemas that we would not interfere was no reason not to follow Rises with the Sun. Dalitha never gave her course of action a second thought, and honestly, neither did I. We paid little attention to the danger we were facing, not because we were feeling so heroic about our cause, but because we knew nothing about all of the forces at work. But then, no one did.

All we knew was that Wolves in Camp and Anna Crow were at Sitting Bull's camp when Sitting Bull was arrested and murdered. What we didn't know was that in the chaos that followed, they fled, as did others. Many of those stragglers departed for the camp of Chief Hump, an old friend of Sitting Bull, where they thought they could find refuge.

But Hump had already determined his people would fight no longer. What's more, he led Sitting Bull's refugees to believe he would fight them himself if they didn't, with him, give themselves up to the bluecoats. So the stragglers moved on west along the White River until they eventually ran into Big Foot's band.

Wolves in Camp had horses, but how many of them he was able to save after the attack at Sitting Bull's camp no one will ever know. I say that because the possibility exists that Anna Crow, very pregnant, might have had to walk long distances, day and night, as the stragglers from Sitting Bull's band fled from danger.

Big Foot, the peacemaker, who told his people more than once that he would never fight again, gave refuge to Anna Crow and Wolves in Camp and the others who'd left Standing Rock, even though those on the run were far more angry than any of Big Foot's own people. They had been—or so Big Foot told the military—starving and ragged when they stumbled into his camp. Big Foot, a man of peace and grace, gave them all refuge—men, women, and children—on December 19.

Just three days later, on their way to Fort Bennett to surrender, Big Foot's band, along with the survivors who'd joined them, marched past their own houses, where Deep Creek joins the Cheyenne River. It was cold and dreary that day, and the sight of their own cabins was too much; they stopped moving toward Fort Bennett, even though Big Foot had promised the bluecoats that they would not. All of this we know now; none of this we knew then.

Big Foot became ill with the grippe that eventually turned into pneumonia. He was in no condition to travel. When his people didn't show up at the fort, Colonel Sumner, who'd trusted Big Foot's word, sent a white civilian the Sioux named Red Beard to warn him and his people that they should get back on the trail to surrender.

Whatever Red Beard told Big Foot in council that day scared them all deeply, and that afternoon, December 23, 1890, Big Foot had his people prepare for a long journey, not to Fort Bennett, but to Pine Ridge, where Red Cloud himself had invited them. That night, in direct violation of military orders and the promise he had given Colonel Sumner, Big Foot, his band, and the stragglers from Standing Rock, began marching south toward Pine Ridge, 150 miles away, in such deep darkness that lanterns had to be lit for them to see the way.

Even today that all-night march is revered by some Sioux in the same way white people esteem the courage of the Pilgrim fathers who left Europe for the freedom to practice their religion. It was their faith that sustained them, people say, and their hunger and the icy blasts of that night's winter wind had little effect as they marched south to what they believed would be their deliverance. Many believed God was on their side, that the spring would bring deliverance, the buffalo, the old ones, the death of the *washechu*. That was their faith. Christ himself had said as much.

Among them, we know now, was Wolves in Camp and Anna Crow. Our friends were there too—Broken Antler and Rises with the Sun. They'd found their daughter in Big Foot's camp, where Deep Creek joins the Cheyenne River. Then they followed the group, maybe three hundred people, on the long march toward Pine Ridge.

Early on the morning of December 26, I quickly packed the wagon and we were off, west and northwest, as Charley had said, on barely distinguishable reservation roads toward the White River. We had no idea what we would find, but Dalitha knew that we had to look for the one who was, as the old hymn says of the lost sheep, "off on the hills away."

The holy man Short Bull and his ghost dancers had long ago left the Rosebud for Pine Ridge, where there were more true believers. In Short Bull's absence and despite the dark shadow of a powerful military buildup, the Rosebud reservation remained calm that warm midwinter. The villages we passed through were remarkably quiet in spite of the general fear everyone felt in the wake of Sitting Bull's murder.

No one knew much about what had happened since Sitting Bull's death almost two weeks before. Dalitha simply wanted to get Anna Crow out of harm's way; she was convinced, like the others, that hostilities were not only possible but practically inevitable. The land was dry and parched, the people starving, the military an ominous presence. The Ghost Dance, on its own, was capable of igniting a prairie fire.

At Little Horse's Camp on Oak Creek we changed directions and headed straight west when the people there told us that some bands of Minneconjou Sioux were on their way to Pine Ridge, even though they'd been ordered not to. They were marching south because they thought they could stay out of harm's way by joining Red Cloud, whom most of the Sioux believed knew best how to get along with *washechu*. We camped that first night somewhere between Oak Creek and Butte Creek. Dalitha was afraid for Anna Crow, but neither of us, as I remember, considered ourselves to be in any immediate danger.

On Saturday, we made it to the Rosebud agency, which had become, by that time, little more than a military fort. Everywhere we looked there were bluecoats. The officers we spoke to considered Big Foot's march south to be in direct violation of orders and a very dangerous threat. We were warned—even commanded—not to keep going west, because any white people on or near the reservation were already leaving, scared to death of what was to come.

My friend Scotty Devans arranged for us to get two fresh horses in place of the wagon, it being clumsy and slow. The next morning, Sunday—the Sabbath—we were on our way, south and west, following the winding path of the Little White River. No one tried to stop us, and in just a few hours we were on the Pine Ridge reservation.

It was now late December, 1890, and still winter was nowhere to be seen. At night, the temperature fell steeply, but during the day the warm west winds brought nothing but clear sky, so the sun, like a king, ruled over the wide plains before us.

What was clear once we'd traveled several hours from the Rosebud agency was that life on Pine Ridge was very different. There were good reasons why some had told us we should not go a mile farther west than Rosebud. Almost every cabin and school stood abandoned.

Somewhere along the way, at a time when the sun already was falling woefully low in the southwestern sky, we came upon a tiny Catholic church. Despite it being Sunday, no one was there. I tied the horses to a tree and walked to the front door. Dalitha was already inside. Fear made me turn back and look over the miles and miles of open space, as if I might spot a column of soldiers or a roving band of Sioux raising clouds of dust from the parched land as they galloped toward us. There was nothing. Then I remember thinking that I was looking only south and west, and that an entire world of danger might still lie behind my back. I stepped back down from the porch and looked behind the church over miles of unbroken space. Nothing.

There I stood, another chicken coop church behind me. Dalitha was inside, but otherwise I was completely alone in this vast empire of uncertain emptiness. I felt very, very small. It seemed to me then—and it still does today—that to live in the middle of such a vast and shapeless world forces you to become a believer. There is nowhere to hide, nowhere to take refuge but in faith. Abraham Brinks, Anna Crow, Dalitha Ward, Arie Boon— we all had to believe something. I wasn't sure where I fit, but it seemed clear to me then that without faith, such emptiness rendered nothing but despair.

I walked into the same kind of church we occasionally attended more than a day's ride back east. The walls were as plain as the grassland around it, the altar something nailed together by the priest maybe, the windows thickly distorted but streaming with the light of midday. Dalitha stood there in a shaft of sunlight. She took one of my hands when I walked to her and then the other, and she prayed aloud. And so did I as the wind whistled through the walls of that clapboard building. That was our worship. That night we slept in the church, our shelter in the time of storm.

# ⚜ Ten ⚜

It was afternoon the next day when we came to the place called Wounded Knee. The sun was gone, hidden away by the so-often-prayed-for blizzard already being announced by thick gray clouds in the sky. We came up from the west, from behind a series of little hills and through a draw or a ravine where there were enough trees to block our view of the horizon. We didn't know where we were exactly— still some distance from the agency at Pine Ridge. But we recognized the fact that the ominous cloud of dust which had appeared before us an hour or two earlier could not have been raised by the wind. We came out of that draw and up on a plain where the world suddenly opened, and that's when we saw what we can neither forget nor ever describe accurately.

The creek called Wounded Knee runs through a broad and shallow valley, maybe a half mile wide, as you know. There's little to distinguish it from any other, except for a bump of a knoll that stands above the ravine to the

218

south. This little hill was the place where the military had rolled their four Hotchkiss guns and aimed them on the encampment below.

I have never seen dead buffalo. I came to the Great Plains after they had been slaughtered by the millions. But when we stopped our horses and looked over that valley, I immediately assumed we'd stumbled on what remained of a buffalo hunt, because everywhere we looked bodies were strewn across the face of the plain, bodies I mistook for buffalo. My imagination was simply incapable of seeing clearly the horror that had happened.

It was a dirty afternoon, the skies full of scudding clouds, winds rising with the upcoming storm. The whole world was almost colorless; nothing was on the horizon but separate shades of ashen gray. Soldiers were walking here and there amid skeletal tipi poles, dead horses, and burned wagons, some of them overturned.

And everywhere, the bodies of the dead. I wasn't capable of thinking at that moment. What I saw—what we saw—is burned into our memories, pictures of hell never to be destroyed or lost, despite what we might like to do with them. I don't think I can explain, but I must try. You want to know the whole story.

Dalitha slapped her horse and took off when she saw something move up ahead. I followed her into the ravine that ran the length of the valley where all the killing had taken place. What we found was a young cavalryman, barely old enough to shave, standing over a fallen Sioux woman clutching her two children, all dead. We were still a half mile at least from the heart of all that death.

Dalitha believes that the Calvinists dwell too much on sin, on depravity, and she may be right. But what I remember in that young soldier's face was nothing more or less than the illumination of evil. His eyes burned like damnation. He had lost reason completely. He raised his rifle toward us when we rode up, and for a moment I thought we too would be dead.

And then something registered in him. Dalitha was white. She was not what he would have called a squaw. A voice he hadn't heard for hours most likely told him not to kill anymore.

There he stood, as I think Cain might have himself, suddenly recognizing his own crime and the bodies of three he'd killed at his feet.

"They came at us," he said, his first words. "They came at us with everything they had." That's what he said, and then he looked down at his feet as if the dead woman and children deserved the result of their own treachery.

It was *their* fault. It was Eve who gave the apple to Adam, and the serpent who had lied.

Of all the images that remain in me from that day, the look on that young man's face as he stood over the dead woman and her children is the one that comes back most often. I have come to believe that the ferocity in his eyes—glowing like the embers of a fire—that ferocity grew from the need to believe that what he'd done could not be judged as wrong, even though the still, small voice of his conscience had already begun to insist otherwise. The ferocity that had exploded in the heat of the battle that had begun in the center of the Wounded Knee encampment was now becoming part of another struggle in the deepest depths of that boy's soul.

Dalitha jumped off her horse, ran to the mother and children, felt for any sign of life, then stood, grabbed the rifle from the boy's hands, took the barrel in hers, and swung it at him, knocking him down. She never said a word. I don't think she could speak.

Dalitha was almost old enough to be his mother, and he knew it. He cried.

I thought we were in hell.

Even today, twenty-five years later, the government will not admit that what happened on December 29, 1890, was a massacre. They call Wounded Knee a battle and Little Big Horn a massacre. But I know the truth. I was there. Even if I was not present the moment it began, I was there when it ended. And it ended, slowly and horribly, sometimes miles away in ravines where women and children were gunned down like animals. I know that, and so do you.

We'd arrived at the very end of the killing, when the formation of troops was already beginning for the trip back to the agency. With the light of day quickly ending, we searched frantically for Anna Crow, Wolves in Camp, Broken Antler, and Rises with the Sun. I could describe pictures I wish I'd never seen as we turned over the mutilated bodies that lay all over the valley. Some were alive and dying; some were alive and would live—but most of them not for long. For years afterward I have remembered that horrible search for four people we were afraid to find, and the odd relief we felt—almost joy, in fact—when the faces we saw belonged to people we didn't know.

I know what it is like, in a kind of panic, to turn over dozens and dozens of dead bodies and grow, in a way, almost callous. That too I will never forget.

Together, we covered as much as we could see of that whole shallow valley, the air cold and shrill with death songs. Some memories should never be resurrected from wherever God gives us grace to bury them.

There at the heart of the encampment, where the fighting had been most vicious, we found Wolves in Camp, his body mangled by the fire of the Hotchkiss guns. Not surprisingly, he'd been in the middle of the fray that morning, like most of the warriors. Even though he was torn by the shot from the Hotchkiss, he looked oddly dignified, at peace. I didn't know him well, and neither did Dalitha, but we thought of him as a very noble young man. Sitting Bull, I think, would have been proud.

Not far away we found our friend from Rosebud, Broken Antler. He too was among those who had fallen in the council circle, where the deadly firing had begun. He was dressed in the only way I'd ever seen him—dark working clothes, like a white man. His hair was short, and there was no paint on him. To me, he was an innocent. Dalitha stopped for a moment, took hold of his lapels, and pulled her face to his chest. He was a wonderful man, a father who'd lost his life trying to save his daughter. You remember, of course, that Dalitha had known and loved Broken Antler and his wife, as well as Anna Crow, a dozen years before she knew her own husband.

Rises with the Sun, like many other women who'd been packing for the trip to the agency, had started to run as soon as the firing began and had slipped down into the ravine, where she'd been shot. Someone else had found her and brought her to the wagon where the Sioux wounded were being kept—and that's where we found her, barely alive. Imagine our joy, even though she wasn't capable of recognizing us. Her wounds were such that she couldn't speak. But the woman we found was Rises with the Sun.

Promise me you will pray you never see anything as God-forsaken as what we saw against the dismal grays of a basinlike valley soaked in dark pools of blood. I grew numb, yet feared that Dalitha's silence, with all those cavalry men around, would explode into some act that would take her, then and there, to her grave. Maybe it was the weight of so many dead that kept her from striking out; maybe it was the fact that so many of the bluecoats themselves seemed unable to understand what had happened. We lived in another world, one all of us wanted to leave. The soldiers too had their dead, many of them carrying their own bullets in their chests, suffering wounds from their own rifles.

More than anything, I think it was Dalitha's determination not to lose any more lives that kept her from screaming. She worked tirelessly that afternoon to find places in the wagons for the Sioux who had been wounded. All the way back—several hours—she stayed beside them in the wagons, bringing, if nothing else, her own body's warmth. She was too busy saving people to think about striking out. If she hadn't been, she could not have ridden back to Pine Ridge amid the columns of bluecoat murderers.

Many of the soldiers seemed completely bewildered. Some of them were immigrants, no more familiar with reservation life than they were with the English language or even riding a horse. A few were actually Seventh Cavalry remnants, Custer's own, veterans of Little Big Horn. Some of them said things I wish I'd never heard; but many seemed as numb as I felt.

It was dark and it was cold all the way back to Pine Ridge, and I remember very little except seeing the newspaperman I'd met at the Ghost Dance.

"So," I said to him, "tonight you will send in your story?"

I don't think he recognized me. He looked up from his horse, as if the two of us shared some secret. "I think we did this to ourselves," he said, and then he looked away. I don't know how he meant me to understand those words, but I won't forget them, because the more they echo in my mind, the more true they seem.

At Pine Ridge, I helped carry pews out of the mission chapel. I helped lug in straw to give the wounded some comfort as they lay on the floor. Dalitha stayed with Rises with the Sun. I will never forget how the wounded who had been taken into the chapel—they were almost entirely women and children—looked away, terrified, if I even glanced at them. I was white.

It wasn't long after that Bishop Hare, a well-known priest who happened to be visiting the reservation, walked into the chapel and nearly fainted at the sight. All around, the walls were hung with long ropes of Christmas greens for the celebration just a few days before, the birth of the Prince of Peace.

Outside, most of the Sioux who'd been staying near the agency quickly departed once they'd heard of the massacre, and the whole place seemed under siege. Occasional shots were fired from out in the hills. I remember some wounded walked in later on foot, having stumbled all the way from Wounded Knee.

I was in the middle of spreading more straw when I stopped beside Dalitha, who'd been helping where she could while closely attending Rises with the Sun. The two of them had hold of each other's hands, and I could see that Rises with the Sun was attempting to speak. Her mouth was moving, even though there were no words. I don't think Dalitha knew I was standing there, but there was something—I don't know what it was—in that moment when I saw them that made me believe Rises with the Sun would not live.

I walked back toward the barn where we'd picked up the straw, and I stood there for a moment, looking east toward Wounded Knee. There was no moon, and there was nothing to see but flakes of snow, a harbinger of the

225

blizzard that finally had come after all our hoping and praying. There were drums, and occasional gunshots rang out as slugs slapped into the wood of the buildings around me. I wasn't afraid. I honestly wasn't afraid, but I don't like to remember any of that because—please listen to me now—because no Buffalo Bill show or dime novels can ever describe the madness I felt living with dark and abiding evil in a world ruled by misrule.

There I stood with no words, only the groaning of my soul, when Dalitha found me. "You have to go," she said. She grabbed me with both her hands and spun me toward her. "You have to go now, before morning. It will be too dangerous later." Her words came in a torrent. "Rises with the Sun says Wolves in Camp sent Anna away in the middle of the night, with a woman, his mother. She says he told her when he awakened her in the darkness. She says he knew somehow that there could be no good at Wounded Knee."

In both of us lay the unspoken realization that when Anna Crow wasn't found among those dragged out of the ravine, she was likely still out there, dead as that mother and her children beneath the feet of the young soldier. For miles in both directions the cavalry had hunted down Big Foot's band—men, women, and children. Even though we'd not said it—it is not always easy to give utterance to one's deepest fears—we assumed Anna Crow would never dance again, nor return to the Rosebud, nor give birth to the child fathered by a man already dead and buried across the Mud.

"She says he told her it was Anna's time and that if she did not go away, it would be a very sad day." Dalitha's face at that moment showed more fear than I had ever seen or would see. "You must go," she said again, and she offered me a heavier coat. I don't know where she got it. She opened it, held it out before me, and I put my arms in. "I don't believe she will see another day," she told me, speaking of Rises with the Sun. "My place is here, with her and with these people who need me. I can speak their language."

"Where?" I asked her.

"Go north and east from Wounded Knee," she told me. And then she kissed me.

Dalitha was risking me for something greater, sacrificing her husband for what was right. Never, I think, were the two of us any closer, even in our separation, because I knew she would just as freely have given herself. I don't know if you understand what I mean, but never were the two of us any more one than we were at that moment.

That's why I was not afraid when I set out in the night. Maybe I can't say it exactly that way—"I was not afraid." I don't think those words describe what I felt as I set out, alone, on my way back to Wounded Knee. Everywhere I looked, fleeting images were stealing in and out of the ravines, scudding across the open fields, and twisting, spiritlike, through snow that swirled like fierce, whitened dancers. Somewhere above, a moon and stars held forth, but swarming snow doused whatever light they might otherwise have thrown over the open plains. Silence and

227

darkness were deceivers—every sound, every motion seemed a gleaming rifle barrel or blade. Shadows wore war paint.

I was afraid when I arrived at that long field of death once again, where even then—it was the middle of the night—figures were moving among the bodies strewn across the face of the earth. I was not alone. I pulled my horse into the shadow of trees south of what had been Big Foot's camp, then dismounted and looked around, all the way around, to be sure I was not being followed. Across the field, a dozen or more Sioux men moved in silence from one body to another. I misspoke when I told you I was not afraid.

For a long time, I walked my horse east on the edge of that ravine, as far down and out of sight as I could get without giving up my ability to see what those men were doing. Their care for their dead and wounded made them oblivious to what was going on around them. Besides, they would not have believed a single white man would chance coming back to the scene of such great horror when, that night especially, outside the agency itself, the reservation belonged to the red man.

I could not stop to ask them about Anna Crow; my deep concern would not have mattered to them. They might have known something I didn't about her condition or her whereabouts, but had I appeared in the middle of what had already become for them a holy place, my sympathies would not have mattered. So I followed the few

228

instructions Rises with the Sun had given Dalitha. I went north and east from Wounded Knee.

Finding Anna Crow, I was convinced, was the right thing to do—not because of Dries Balkema's dying pledge or his parents' belief in the covenant, but because with Wounded Knee behind her, Anna Crow was far more alone in this world than she'd ever been as a teacher on the Rosebud, at the boarding school before that, or certainly with the dancers and Big Foot's band just a day before. That shine in her eyes, her faith in Wovoka's vision, her belief in Jesus Christ's second coming to relieve the suffering of her people—all of that faith, I knew, must have died at Wounded Knee. I was afraid that night, but I was less important than she was. One of the gifts of faith is a selflessness that diminishes fear.

From the south, I circled the wide space where blackened tipi poles seemed like crosses over the burial ground, and kept moving until I spotted the dim light in a cabin barely a mile east. The snow was coming harder. I knew I couldn't be seen even close up, so when I came nearer I hid my horse in a stand of trees and walked to the side of the cabin and the nearest window.

Anna Crow was not inside. I don't know that I counted the number of those who were, but half of them at least— all Sioux—appeared dead, men and women. Some moved. Some were alive. Some had dragged themselves away from death, only to find it there with a roof over their heads. It was a cabin without a wood floor, and the dirt had turned inky with blood.

Was it right of me to go on, to continue to search for a young woman when others were dying in that cabin? Did I leave because Anna Crow was carrying a baby whose father was white? For years afterward, when I'd come upon a deserted cabin on the reservation, I'd think of what I saw through the window that night and ask myself whether or not I was right to keep searching. But today I'm older, and one of the comforts of age is that, unlike the young, we begin to live more humbly with unanswered questions. That may be what my people call "sanctification."

I went on, but what I saw through that window has never left me.

It was dark and dangerous, and Pine Ridge at that time of night had endless shadowy lines where trees ran across the open plains and up and down the buttes like the darkened feathers of an old flowing headdress. You know that wide land, and by now I hope you know me well enough to understand the reverence I intend for what I am about to say, because there are few events in my life about which I can say so assuredly that God Almighty directed my path. I tried to follow what I assumed—but could only guess—might be the path Anna Crow and the mother of Wolves in Camp had taken the night before as they fled north and east. They left no tracks; there had been no snow the night before. I stuck to the rutted road and the trampled grasses where Big Foot's band, surrounded by cavalry, had made their way south and west to the valley of the Wounded Knee, but I had no idea, no idea at all, where Anna might be.

230

Twice I walked quietly up to darkened log cabins where there was no light from a fire inside. Both times I crept away again, assuming that if the occupants were asleep inside—and if Anna Crow was one of them—for the time being at least, everything was all right. Once, I spotted a band of Sioux galloping toward the Wounded Knee, which was, by then, four or five miles behind me. It was not a night to see or hear things well, and they passed without seeing the lone *washechu*.

What I am saying is that I am convinced God brought me to her. It is too amazing a coincidence to think otherwise. The two of them could have simply kept traveling and been miles ahead of me. They could have gone off into a stand of pines almost anywhere in that wide and dark world. But I suspected that they'd tried to find shelter somewhere, so I looked for cabins and shacks, and finally, amazingly, I found them.

# ⚞ *Eleven* ⚟

Anna Crow was in a cabin at the base of Porcupine Butte. I saw her through the window—although when I remember looking inside, I don't believe I could have recognized her right away. A buffalo robe was thrown over her, and she lay near a little fire that lit the east side of the cabin. Her face was turned away, and even if I could have recognized the ghost shirt she was wearing, I didn't see it when I looked through that frosted window. What I saw instead was a baby wrapped in the arms of a woman who was staring into the fire, rocking slightly and singing. Through the walls, I couldn't hear her song, but I watched her lips move.

Across the room sat a man with a Winchester across his lap. He was guarding them, alone. He wasn't sleeping, but the warmth, the fear of the long day, the song of the woman, and the relief at the fact that the baby had finally arrived—all of that may well have conspired to make him less than watchful. Out back of the cabin I'd seen the outlines of a fence around a garden, a wagon up beside the lean-to; he was likely a progressive—perhaps he'd begun to do what even Red Cloud had suggested, and put away some of the old life. If that was true, then that night he was likely afraid of everyone—both the whites who'd massacred Big Foot's band, and Sioux who would look at his goats or his cows or whatever he had and see a traitor. He had reason to fear everyone. That's why he had the rifle.

I considered leaving. The woman with the baby was proof enough of things having gone well. Besides, the man with the gun considered himself an enemy of anyone walking into his house. If I were to knock, he would fire.

The woman put down the baby on a blanket beside her, got to her knees, and shuffled toward Anna Crow. Carefully, she pulled back the robe—very carefully, too carefully. Then she lifted the blankets until she uncovered enough of Anna's body for me to see blood everywhere. She took the dry ends of the blankets and shoved them under the girl, then wrapped her up again.

What I saw in that act was the jagged outlines of a death I had seen all too well years ago on the night of my greatest grief. I saw Anna Crow—and I didn't, because I saw my wife, my first wife.

There were no hospitals near the village where we'd lived on the shores of Lake Michigan, and we were very poor. We had far more than this progressive farmer at the foot of Porcupine Butte, but with gas lamps and candles shedding the only available light, the corners of his cabin were just as dark and fearful as what I couldn't help but remember of that night years before. Maybe it was because of Rinska that I recognized—I simply knew—that Anna's condition was dangerous. There she lay, as had my wife, in the middle of the room, no one able to do anything. Not even God, it seemed.

Blood flowing from a body has effects that go beyond reason, but I had more than enough cause to act immediately. Just a bit earlier, I had thought that if I were to find Anna Crow, God himself would have to direct me to her. He had. I stood at the window of a tiny cabin at the base of Porcupine Butte with Anna Crow looking far too much like the woman whose life I'd once lost, a woman I once loved. I had to stay, and I had to help. The only way to get into that cabin was by sheer force.

I crept around the front to the door, pulled out my pistol, kicked that door in, then charged inside and grabbed the rifle off the man's lap before anyone could move.

Terror bled from his eyes, but the woman who'd been tending Anna Crow didn't look at me. Instinctively, she scrambled for the baby.

For a moment I stood there. I saw fear in both of their eyes; the man, middle-aged like myself, still sitting on the floor of the cabin; the woman holding the baby, telling me with her eyes that I would have to kill her to get the child.

I held my Colt in one hand, the rifle in the other. I sat down, crossed the rifle over my lap, as he had, and stuck the pistol back into my coat. "Anna Crow," I said, pointing at the woman wrapped in blankets close to the fire. Astonishment appeared in the woman's face. "Jan Ellerbroek," I said, pointing at my chest, and then I said again, still pointing, "Anna Crow."

No one moved.

The rifle was my only way of telling them that I meant no harm. I showed it plainly to both of them, then gave it back to the man who sat beside me. He wouldn't move, wouldn't take it. I laid it across his lap, then sat back and held both hands out in front of me, as if to say I was not interested in hurting them.

When he grabbed the Winchester, I could see in the dim light thrown by the small fire that his face showed more curiosity than anger.

"From Rosebud." I pointed again at myself. "Sister Ward is my wife," I said, hoping her name would spark some recognition. "Many are dead at the Wounded Knee," I said, even though I was sure they already knew. "Many of your people are gone." Once again, I pointed. "Anna Crow is our friend."

The woman looked down at the baby in her arms. Her lips tightened. She looked at the man holding the rifle, then once again at me.

"The baby—is good, is healthy?" I asked, motioning toward my own throat and chest.

I tried not to show any fear as the man positioned the rifle. I knew he could shoot me, and he knew it too.

"We want to know that the baby is good," I told them. "We are her friends from Rosebud." I pointed again at the bundled woman in the blankets. "We are friends. Sister Ward is my wife. Sister Ward is the teacher."

The woman looked again at the man with the rifle. Then she looked down at the child, pulled back the blankets, and glanced at its face.

"It is girl or boy?" I said, and then she came to me. I was seated on the floor. Once again she looked at the man with the rifle, as if to be sure he was able to defend them all. She stooped beside me, holding the child in her arms, and opened the blankets for me to see the baby's face.

That's when I saw you for the very first time. You were beautiful. New life is—always. Believe me. In the desolation all around us, in the smoke of battle that seemed forever trapped in my nostrils, after the horror I'd seen that day at Wounded Knee, and the agony in the chapel, the bodies all over that field, the midnight snow driving all around—amid all of that, your face, your innocence in sleep, your beauty, your life itself was a miracle. It was simply a miracle.

I don't know if you understand what I'm trying to tell you, but at that moment, I believe that you, a baby no more than an hour old, saved something of my life, even though it was my charge and my calling to try somehow to save you. This is your story, Touches the Sky, but you understand now why it is mine as well. Seeing you was more precious than I can ever tell you, even today, more precious than you will ever imagine.

You have asked me to tell you the story, what I know about your birth and what I know of how it was you came into this world. Your face was round and red, and you were asleep in the arms of a woman I'd never seen before, a woman who would have given her life for yours. You were a perfect, trusting child who knew nothing at all about the death you had just escaped because a man named Wolves in Camp had a vision of what would happen on the creek called Wounded Knee.

"It is girl," the woman said.

"Yes," I said. I reached out my arms, not because I wanted so badly to hold you, but because I wanted them to believe that I meant neither them, nor you, nor your mother any harm.

Once again she looked at the man with the rifle, and he nodded. She looked at me in the way very few Sioux women ever have; she wanted to know if what was in my eyes was really love. She said one word, not to him, but to me. "Friend," she said, and she gave you to me.

When I held you that first time, you were my own children, buried in the earth many miles away; you were every child, red and white; you were the gift of life amid darkness and storm and death. You were a child who would be named Touches the Sky. You were a child of hope.

I can't say I thought it all in so many words, but I can tell you this: While I am not a man of visions, not a holy man, something in me was healed at the moment you were in my arms. Something had come full circle.

237

The woman pointed at your mother, then shook her head, and I understood that she meant to tell me your mother was dying.

It was the man who spoke. "She does not want to live," he said.

"The bleeding?" I said.

He nodded. "She will not eat. She will not drink."

I gave you back to the woman, then got on my knees and crept over the floor closer to the fire, to Anna Crow. Her color was ashen, and her eyes seemed sunken. She did not appear to be awake. I touched her cheek and found her cold. I put my hand in front of her face to feel her breath. It was still there.

Just minutes before, I'd seen the woman change the blankets. I'd seen the blood. I looked back up at her and opened the blankets again because I wanted to see something of the volume of the bleeding. Judging from the color of her face and her sleepiness, I thought she had likely already lost a lot of blood. The flow had slowed, though—that's what I believed. But the man had said she wouldn't eat or drink. Your mother did not want to live.

The truth, Touches the Sky, is that your mother loved you—that you know. But then, at the moment she gave you her greatest gift, she could see only utter darkness all around. That too, I understand, as do you.

"Anna," I said.

There was no sign of life on her face.

"Anna," I said again.

238

Nothing moved. Nothing changed. Nothing in her face seemed to respond.

I rubbed her face lightly, smoothed back her hair, held my warm hand over her forehead, pulled the blankets away a bit and touched her neck, rubbed it with my fingers. I said her name again, but there was no reaction in her face. I held my hand in front of her nose and lips, bent my own face to hers to see if I could feel breath.

She was a woman dying in childbirth. Another woman dying in childbirth.

"He wanted you to live," I told her. I was close enough to her face to see every possible movement. "Wolves in Camp—he wanted you, more than anything, to live. You remember that. He sent you away because he knew what would happen, and he wanted you to live."

Beneath those blankets she was lying on her back, her body less than warm. I rubbed her shoulders, her arms, her hands. "Sister Ward sent me to find you," I told her. "We were at the agency. There are many suffering. She had to stay." I told her my name. I told her something of what had happened. I told her once again that Sister Ward had told me to find her. "She wants you to live."

The woman held out a cup of water.

"I'll lift you now," I told her, "because you need to drink. All of us want you to drink. Sister Ward wants you to drink. Wolves in Camp wants you to drink. I, Jan Ellerbroek, want you to drink. These friends who have saved your life too—all of us want you to drink."

Her eyes fluttered.

I did as I had promised. I reached beneath her with my right arm, pulled her up slightly, and wrapped my arm around her so that the woman could come close enough to offer the cup and tip it to Anna's lips until water ran down the sides of her face into the blankets.

"You must drink," I said. "The water is life. You must drink."

Not once had her eyes opened, but her face twitched, her breath came more forcefully.

"You have a beautiful daughter," I said. "You must drink the water."

She would not. It spilled off her face and onto my hands as I held her.

The woman took back the cup and looked away.

I could not let Anna Crow die.

I had not studied medicine. I was not a doctor. But I had seen more than enough of death in my life, and what I saw that night in Anna Crow's refusal to drink, in her sallow face, her grayness, her cold skin, was something that I'd known all too well many years before.

The man must have put down the rifle, because when the woman took the water cup away from Anna's mouth, he was holding you, there across the room. Anna Crow was in my arms, and I was rubbing her arms and hands, trying to awaken her limbs, trying to do with my hands what I hadn't been able to do with words. The woman brought you to your mother, who was sitting up in my arms. You were asleep, and you were clean, wrapped in a shirt and a foxskin.

The woman spoke to Anna Crow in the Sioux language, and the man, who'd come closer now, told me what she said. It was about you—about how beautiful you were, about how the Great Spirit had wanted you not to die, about how you would need your mother. Anna Crow's arms were wrapped up in the blankets, but the woman kneeled near enough so that when your mother's eyes fluttered and opened, all they could see was your face.

And then she spoke, your mother. She spoke in the Sioux language. She said you had no father.

The woman told her that the father was the Great Mystery.

Your mother looked at me. "Then she has no need of me," she said, again in Sioux. Then she said to me, in English, "It is a good day to die. I will die with my people."

"These are your people too," I told her. "Anna, this baby is yours."

"They are dead—they are all dead. I know."

"Your baby is alive," I said.

"Let God have her then. Let the Great Spirit have his way."

Once, years ago, before I'd left Michigan, my father told me people sometimes die from despair. Even if they still breathed, inside they were dead. When your mother said what she did—"Let the Great Spirit have his way"—I knew what it was that was killing your mother. Her spirit was dying because her faith was gone.

So how could I speak to her of Jesus Christ? Jesus Christ had come to Wovoka and told him that heaven

241

would return if only they would dance. Jesus Christ, she would have said, could have her daughter too. Jesus Christ, like the Great Spirit, had vanished from her soul.

No preacher's words could have touched her. Not even her own beautiful daughter could arouse the will to live within her. The man had been right from the very beginning: Anna Crow did not want to live.

I could not give your mother my blood, but I could give my heart. So this is what I told her. "Anna Crow, you know Sister Ward. You know her because always she has been good to you, good to your people."

Her eyes were closed. I held her in my arms. I embraced her. I kept moving my hands across her shoulders, but I think she was willing her spirit away.

"She has been good to me too, Sister Ward. Once I thought all that was good was buried somewhere beneath the ground. Once I saw people smile and laugh, and thought such joy could never be mine again." And then I said, "Are you listening to my voice?"

She didn't move.

"Anna Crow, you must let me tell you this story," I said. "Once in another life I buried two children and a woman I loved more than life itself. Once I was sure that joy had left me alone in the darkness." I shook her softly in my hands. "Don't you go away, Anna Crow. Don't go away until you hear me."

Her head moved just slightly.

"Once I thought—like you—that the skies were empty, that the land was dry and broken, that the sun was just

242

a dream. I know what it means to feel empty in the soul—I know. With my own hands, I buried everything I loved."

That's what I told her. I could not let her die.

"Today," I said, "I have Sister Ward. Listen to me, Anna Crow. Today, Sister Ward smiles, and joy has come back in my life. I know that for you, just as there was for me, there is reason to despair. But there is always reason to hope. Listen to me, because I know."

And then, once again, she opened her eyes.

"God has lied," she said.

"We lie to ourselves. But he is always with us."

"How do you know?" she asked.

"Because I'm here," I told her. "Because I'm a man who has been at such a place before. I've known death like my own face in a mirror. But I know too that joy hasn't departed forever."

"Here?" she said.

"Yes," I told her. "Right here. He has blessed me with you." And then I prayed. "Take Anna Crow into your arms, Lord. Take her in your arms." That was the prayer. No more.

She looked at me, her eyes faint and worn, then closed them and fell back into something like sleep.

"Anna," I said, "you must drink." I took her chin in my hand and pinched it. "I'm going to give you water again, and you must drink."

The woman returned. We held the cup up to Anna's face. We tipped it slightly, and once again the water ran down her cheeks. And then the woman said something in the Sioux language, and Anna Crow lifted her eyes once more. This time, for the first time, I saw a questioning, a glint of something curious, hopeful.

I looked at the man across the room. "She told her that many are praying," he said. "Even the dead are praying."

"God wants you to live," I told Anna Crow.

Once more, the woman raised the water to your mother's lips, and this time—give thanks to God—she drank. This time some of it went into her thirsty body and her parched soul.

And now, I've come to understand, myself, something of what happened that night, not so much in your mother, who decided with that drink of water that she would live, but in myself, in my own thirsty body and parched soul. I don't know that our Father in heaven makes deals with us—this for that, that for this—but I know he gave me faith once again that night by letting me be something of his voice in a time and a place where death stalked just outside. I held a young mother in my arms, and she'd come to live. It was not a trade, but when I think about that night, I know what happened was an answer to a question that had burned like a fire for far too long in my soul. I was God's servant, even in my unbelief.

I told your mother that God had brought me to her, but now—these many years later—I am just as confident that he brought her and you to me.

Your mother lived because she wanted to, because Wolves in Camp protected her from the massacre at Wounded Knee, because his mother wouldn't let her die. But most of all, Touches the Sky, I want you to know I believe God Almighty was the one who wouldn't let Anna Crow go that night. He had his reasons.

You wanted to know, you said, what I knew about the story of your birth. You said your mother told you that maybe the only one who knows it all is a man named Jan Ellerbroek. You wrote me a letter that said your mother had wanted you to ask. What I've told you is the story, from the very heart of my soul.

# ⇥ Twelve ⇤

After the massacre, lots of sad and angry things happened on the reservation. Even the peaceful Sioux left the agency to try to figure out what had happened. They lived, for a time, in fear of their lives. Places like the small cabin where you were born were plundered when those who were most hostile took revenge for the tragedy on people like the man whose name I don't even remember, the man who put down his rifle when I put it in his hands.

I made it back to the agency a couple of days later. I had stayed in the cabin until I was sure that things were under control. You were well cared for, as was your mother.

The snow had come to cover the horror with a blanket of white—something the Sioux thought to be a shroud from the God of the whites, something to cover their sin. When I passed the place where the encampment had been, white men were pillaging what was left, taking the ghost shirts off the dead to keep or sell as mementos.

246

When I saw one of them by himself—a fat man with a big mustache—I rode up to him on my horse. It never dawned on him that I would be anything other than a scavenger. I got off my horse and simply knocked him down with my fist, grabbed the shirt from his hands, and stuck it in my saddlebag. I didn't want him to have it.

Dalitha was happy to see me, even though most of the patients she and the others had cared for had died or were dying. Only after I had gone, she told me, did she come to understand how dangerous it had been for me to go out there just after the massacre. "If I had known," she said.

I told her that had she known, it wouldn't have made any difference.

"You didn't bring them back," she said. It wasn't a question.

I told her things would be fine. She didn't need to hear the whole story just then. I simply told her I'd found Anna Crow and a new baby girl, and I believed that things would be fine.

There is a marker today on the same hill from which four Hotchkiss guns rained death on Big Foot's encampment at Wounded Knee. You may have seen it. That marker lists the names of just a few of those who are buried in a mass grave on that same hill. The name of Wolves in Camp and that of your grandfather, Broken Antler, are not listed. But Dalitha and I know that both of them perished there, with many others.

Rises with the Sun, like so many of those who were taken back to the agency after the massacre, lived just a

47

few days before succumbing to her wounds. Dalitha was with her when she died.

My father died in Michigan several years later, and when the telegram came telling us of his unexpected death, I went east on the train. Much had needed to be said between us, but it never was. I think, though, that the last moment we saw each other in Harrison was enough for him to believe that his wayward son's eternal future was secure. My father never saw visions, but that doesn't mean he was not a holy man.

The parents of your father, Mr. and Mrs. Balkema, lived in one of those big houses Mr. Balkema had built. That's where I visited them the year my father died. I told them I had every reason to believe their granddaughter was alive and well somewhere on the Standing Rock reservation, as that was where your mother went to live with the Hunkpapa Sioux, the people of Wolves in Camp. Perhaps I should have told them of Wounded Knee and what had happened on Porcupine Butte, but I did not.

My mother died eight years after my father. In the years following his death, she lived with my brother in the parsonage beside his church in a small town in Michigan. I went to her funeral too. I don't know that she ever understood how it was that her son could live so comfortably in so backward a place. She used to write beautiful letters, as much to Dalitha as to me.

Arie Boon was killed in an accident on the farm northwest of what used to be Friesland, South Dakota. Occasionally, I see his wife, who has moved to Platte. Once, years ago, she told me she suspected that Dries Balkema had taken his own life. He had been rejected by his girl-friend, would become the father of a child he would never see, was employed by a man difficult to respect, and had broken with his family hundreds of miles away.

Maybe no one will ever know exactly what did happen to your father. Those were restless, lawless days on the Mud. Maybe Mrs. Boon savors the possibility of his self-inflicted death because she needs to cover her own fear that Balkema and her husband had quarreled violently. Claiming that Dries took his own life made Arie Boon look much better than he might have been. After all, he chose to blame the hostiles and thereby saved Dries from the shame that suicide would have brought upon his mem-ory in the community. But I must say this much for Arie Boon—he did tell us about you. He did not have to. Your story would be something other than what I've told you without him.

So much changed with the coming of the railroad. For the most part, my employment as a drayman was nearly over as the rails delivered commodities all over South Dakota. When Harrison didn't get the railroad, businesses moved. Friesland, Edgerton, Castalia, Nieveen—eventu-ally they either dried up or people pulled up stakes and moved into what is now Platte, South Dakota.

Dalitha and I moved south and west when unceded land on the reservation was opened and sold. We now live several miles south of the Rosebud agency, and when the rains come, I harvest crops, mostly hay. When we get no rain, we get no crop. That's what life is like out here, but you know that.

Dalitha teaches children at St. Francis Mission, but she is not Roman Catholic. It's a secret that is well known. We were, perhaps, married too late to have our own children; but that doesn't mean our farmhouse is empty. Her schoolchildren frequently visit.

She could never leave the reservation, and I could never leave her. So we bought reservation land near a place where a number of people from Charles Mix and Douglas County homesteaded, a place we call Purewater, because an ocean of water lies magnificently beneath a land often too parched for crops. That's where we go to church. This one is block, not frame, but still, by Eastern standards, little more than a chicken coop.

This land, as you know, is harsh and difficult. Today I scratch the earth like so many Sioux would not, but what I plant is subject always to whims of weather that can bless us with soft rain or starve us with drought and wind. Sometimes in July, when the corn is knee-high and green as emerald, a hot, dry wind will scorch a season's bounty in two hours. Winter cold can freeze limbs in minutes, but some Januarys can be as warm as May.

On our land, you can see almost forever. Some people joke that out here a man can watch his dog run away for three days. Storms signal their coming with raised fists; dust turns the whole world dirty gray. But some mornings, in the dawn's golden touch, the sky is a taste of heaven's joy. Some mornings in all this open space, I can,

James Calvin Schaap

like nowhere else, find myself near unto God. But you live here too. You know what I mean.

Two miles south of where we live a small butte rises from the flat land, maybe two acres of a tabletop thirty feet or so above the surrounding grassland. It is a holy place. Young Sioux men go there to see their visions, as they have for many years.

Some of the people in our church at Purewater think I should keep the Sioux from going there, because what it is they practice is a false religion. Some believe that the Brule people will not progress until they become the good Christians we think we are. Some shake their heads at Dalitha and me; they think we're too close to the Indian people.

I don't go up there anymore. I used to. It is, after all, my land. But it is also a sacred place for the Sioux, a place where I have no place.

It seems to me that if my life and yours teach anything, it is that God Almighty wants our will, not only our fear, not only our spiritual ecstasy, not only our feelings, not only our joyful hope. He wants all of us. He wants us from inside out. He wants us to want him. So I try to be what I am, a believer in Christ's love and his atonement; and I let the Sioux be, waiting on God's call. I try to love as God has loved me, and when I can, I say only as much as these friends of mine will hear.

I know this story has gone on too long. Dalitha says I have written a book. I didn't intend it, but maybe a quarter century is enough time for what I can't forget to simmer into something I can explain, a story I can now tell.

251

Your mother, you say, lived a hard life at Standing Rock. I remember the radiance of her faith in Wovoka's vision, and it is difficult for me to imagine that living with a history of such broken dreams could ever have been easy for her. But I doubt that stealing you away the night I first saw you and delivering you as a baby to a big house in Michigan would have been the right thing to do. God wants our wills, but that doesn't mean he doesn't give us our stories.

And I want you to know this as well, Touches the Sky—your letter has meant a great deal to me, as you can see by these many pages of scribbles. It is an answer to many prayers that were made for you for many years. Twice we saw you when Anna Crow returned to the Rosebud to visit with relatives. You were beautiful, light-skinned like so many mixed bloods on the reservation. You were a precious child, and you still are. So many risked their lives that you should live. You have a destiny, Touches the Sky. You have an eternal future. Just as your mother and Dalitha and Wolves in Camp and Broken Antler and Rises with the Sun—and Abraham Brinks and Arie Boon and my father and mother—all have eternities. Your mother's people know better than your father's how time is really a delusion.

Dalitha says not to preach. She has read every word I've written and changed some. She has remembered what I have forgotten. Our stories—and part of yours—are tied together tightly.

In a separate package I am sending the ghost shirt, the one I took from the white man pillaging the dead at Wounded Knee. It is not mine and never was. It is yours.

It is wonderful to know that your mother asked you to write to us before she died, that she wanted us to know that it was well with her soul, and that she wanted you to know this story which has been so long in telling. It is sad to think of her being gone. Dalitha and I, we are both very sorry for you and mourn your loss.

I know this, Touches the Sky—I know this world can be hard. I know that, in part, it is, as the Scriptures say, a vale of tears. I have seen enough of death in my life to know that our joys here are as dependent on the seasons as are the crops I sow every spring. Rough winds can kill. Tornadoes dance across these prairies like pillars of death. Winter's cold freezes life stiff and unyielding. Prairie fires, even today, burn out homesteads as if they were little more than cord wood.

But I live here because it is my home. And what gives me life amid the changing seasons, the trials and joys, the death and the new life, is what I remember always, unseen, beneath us—a deep and life-giving sea of pure water, an ocean of life that is always there in our deepest need.

This I know. God is here. This I know, Touches the Sky.

You are very welcome to visit, trust me. We will greet you with open arms, Dalitha and I. Please do. Please do.

Jan Ellerbroek<br>Purewater, South Dakota

**James Calvin Schaap** is a professor of English at Dordt College in Iowa, and his work continues to receive acclaim and attention. He's the author of more than twenty books, including his novels *Romey's Place, The Secrets of Barneveld Calvary*, and *In the Silence There Are Ghosts*. His articles, essays, and short stories have appeared in magazines, journals, and anthologies.